THE ODYSSEY OF THE AOR

(Architect of Record)

by Jimmy Chelta pseudonymously

iUniverse®

THE ODYSSEY OF THE AOR
(ARCHITECT OF RECORD)

iUniverse books may be ordered through booksellers or by contacting:

iUniverse
1663 Liberty Drive
Bloomington, IN 47403
www.iuniverse.com
1-800-Authors (1-800-288-4677)

ISBN: 978-1-4917-8157-9 (sc)
ISBN: 978-1-4917-8159-3 (hc)
ISBN: 978-1-4917-8158-6 (e)

Library of Congress Control Number: 2015920071

Print information available on the last page.

iUniverse rev. date: 01/22/2016

Disclaimer

Please excuse typos, misspellings, inflections, malapropisms and anything else that might be considered an abuse of the English language.

The following is an unexpurgated and semi-edited stream of consciousness typed using the two finger hunt and peck method.

Intentionally omitted is a glossary of definitions. If you encounter an unfamiliar word, please resort to your nearby mobile device and access a search engine (preferably 8 cylinder, turbo charged).

If you are without a mobile device, please use the old standard but always reliable dictionary.

This story is pure fiction and any resemblance it may have to any persons is completely without intent or malice and the author bears no responsibility for what may be construed as reality.

Thank you

INTRODUCTION

I have found the process of real estate development fascinating as well as, sometimes, entertaining, so I decided to write this story about the amusing characters and processes that come together to build a residential condominium.

I have attended and participated in countless meetings, taking copious notes and minutes of the colorful and diverse personalities, recollected the various roles of the stakeholders, their conversations and positions of brinksmanship, now embellished together in this story.

Real estate development is a risky undertaking and fraught with complex issues. There are so many factors, some controllable and some not, all of which play into the guaranteed uncertain success of real estate development. Some of these factors are naturally human, some purely physical. Mix hubris, inflated egos, greed, false sense of reality, location, market trends, land costs, construction costs, targeted audience, price pointing, contractors' reliability, money lenders, hyperbole of real estate brokers, attorneys and on and on and with that you've got the composition ingredients for real estate development.

What makes a development a winner is simple, it makes money. What makes a development a loser is also simple, it loses money. Not unlike roulette, playing the slots or betting the horses, real estate development can be compared to an intense form of gambling but with much higher stakes and a significantly longer waiting time for success or failure.

The Odyssey of the AOR (an acronym for the Architect of Record) is a satire about an architect's participation in the fictional development of a residential condominium. The names are of course fabricated and have been exaggerated for effect and humor but the underlying story is true to real-world real estate development. It's based on actual experiences I've had as an architect hired by real estate developers. The role of the AOR is to take Schematic Plans (Concept Plans) often developed by an overrated but sometimes famous architect (called by many a Starchitect) and prepare requisite Design Development Documents and Construction Documents for acquiring a building permit and then participate in the daily construction process by answering questions from contractors and making frequent site visits as the building gets built. Most developers pay handsome fees to a Starchitect for their name recognition that goes with the marketability of their project, while the AOR labors without comparable compensation or very much public recognition, being responsible in perpetuity for the integrity and coordination of building systems, life safety and remaining exposure to potential future lawsuits. .

So sit back, buckle up and enjoy the twists and turns of this raucous and somewhat raunchy journey of the AOR swimming in the development shark tank containing an egomaniacal developer, a narcissistic Starchitect and a cast of characters worthy of poking fun at.

To the cognoscenti, the term 'StarArchitect' - or 'Starchitect' – (a title given to designers of world-class luxury condominiums) - is not only well known, but often is used to establish social status at upper crust urban cocktail parties.

"HaaRumphh. Felicity and I have decided to buy an apartment in a building developed by Jon Arrea and designed by the bespoke Star Archie-tek, Les Ismore; it's absolutely fantastic. Amazingly, everything has been thought of. The faux marble's been imported from Morocco and the flooring has a special covering which never needs waxing; the housekeeper will never have to get down and bend over on her hands and knees. It's truly amazing; incredible bathrooms –superlatives abound!"

Felicity's husband Farouk doesn't mention that he also pays for a lower eastside apartment where his twenty five year old weekly girlfriend lives – but that's beside the point. Buffy, cosmopolitan cocktail in hand – listening – is quite impressed. Her husband, Headly, is thinking about the housekeeper bent over on her hands and knees.

And the developer, Jon Arrea, has recently declared bankruptcy.

And so it goes.

Developing residential buildings is not for the faint of heart. It is the 'shark tank' of business environments where most developers swim in the currents of demographic changes and trends and remain ready to 'chomp down' on the rich blood of any potential development opportunity. Developers have to act and navigate quickly. Quickly is having a vision, tying up the land, understanding – or trying to - applicable zoning and building code regulations, working with money lenders, figuring out what they can build and assembling a team who ostensibly know what they're doing – while consistently keeping an eye on the potential return of their investment and constantly being aware that other developers with rows of razor sharp teeth, who are equally savvy or more so, are trying to trump the other for the same property and so forth and so on. Development can be a torn-up, pothole littered highway strewn with roadkill.

As witness to the population shifts to live in cities, plus with the great influx of foreign money used in the United States as a safe place to invest, the response is the development of many more residential condominium buildings with each developer extolling the virtues of his building, while at the same time trying to outdo developments competing for buyers. Since the pace of creating more urban, multi-story housing has intensified, developers of these building types are now faced with the extraordinary task of creating profile condominium residences where the apartment units in their buildings will be in great demand and using a Starchitect's name helps elevate its publicity value.

The term 'Starchitect' reflects the superficial zeitgeist in which it was coined. It was conjured up by marketing, real estate brokers and branding savants who work for residential developers. The 'Starchitect' is generally a stylist based on media hyperbole and somewhat analogous to the designer of trendy blue jeans that are currently sold pre-torn, pre- worn and marketed to hipsters at a premium cost versus an original pair of functional, sturdy dungarees.

A great architect of which there are many, both past and present and a few who are even visionary, creates beautiful, provocative buildings combining art, engineering, the environment, technological innovation and a host of many other considerations. Frank Lloyd Wright -- a great architect, never known as a Starchitect - was an original dungaree. A Starchitect is synonymous with the fashion designer of new pre-torn pair of 'cool' blue jeans destined to go out of style.

But to residential condominium developers, using a Starchitect's name is absolutely essential. It's as essential as the hood ornament on a car. I doubt more than a few could identify the make of a car if it was stripped of its logo and name. As a side note, interestingly enough, years ago, an automobile could easily be identified by its unique styling. Not so today! Sameness, style copying and lack of creativity has reduced many automobiles to relying on marketing the name and sometimes its storied history, if it had one, to establish its social stature. It's very much the same, for the most part, with residential buildings.

A developer who wants to bring a certain level of credibility and panache to his project does so by using the name of a Starchitect even if the parcel of land it's to be built on is listed as an environmental waste hazard. The role of the 'Starchitect' in such a project is usually relegated to just designing the exterior and might include apartment layouts and finishes, irrespective of what the building cost overruns that might result from the Starchitect's decisions on materials and what subsequently follows in the efforts to bring the project back into budget.

So by using the name of a Starchitect, the developer knows potential buyers will be impressed since most people are impressed with names. Think for just a moment how important a name is. Earlier I mentioned Frank Lloyd Wright. Would you buy an apartment in a building designed him? Of course you would. What about a building designed by Hitler's favorite, Albert Speer? Can you imagine the response - at that same cocktail party mentioned on the first page - where Farouk would say to a fashionably, thinly dressed guest named Asparagus (who hides her Jewish heritage) – "We just bought an apartment in the Albert Speer building"? Asparagus' reaction would then be directed to Bunny, the host: ***"Dah-ling: Where's the closest 'baahthroom' – I'm feeling a little faint and might toss my cookies."***

In this story, Sy Philis is the residential developer with grandiose aspirations to build the all-time biggest and best condominiums. He has a reputation as the worst of slum lords since all of his housing projects are rife with problems, which in turn effects his social status. Forget the elite, exclusive social clubs he can't get into; Sy's not even invited to join a local motorcycle gang. But he wants to be recognized as a highly regarded developer, become a 'respected name' and hopefully get accepted to a private club of renowned and restricted stature.

Sy knows the value of using the name of a Starchitect, so he seeks out Les Ismore, known for his highly publicized residential projects, his social connections and known to the fashionistas as a Starchitect.

The beginning of the relationship between Sy Philis and Les Ismore starts with a simple phone call and goes as follows:

"Good morning, Ismore Architects, Framunda speaking."

Secretary for Sy says: "Mr. Philis would like to speak with Mr. Ismore about a project."

Framunda: "Please hold – I'll see if Mr. Ismore is available."

The brinksmanship first starts with the initial communication.

"Les Ismore speaking."

"Please hold for Mr. Philis."

Two minutes of silence pass and then Ismore hangs up.

Phone at Ismore's office rings again.

"Good morning, Ismore Architects, Framunda speaking."

Secretary on phone: "I apologize for the disconnection, please hold for Mr. Philis."

30 seconds pass; Ismore is getting impatient.

"Les, it's Sy Philis. I heard about the project you designed for Jon Arrea. 85% sold within one week. Wow! I'm impressed. How 'bout doing a project for me – let's do lunch."

Sy and Les agree to meet the following week at a chic restaurant.

Sy's turned out in a $6,000 custom made suit, loosley fitting (hair) rug, oversized gold framed sunglasses, heavy face tan makeup and a complete set of poorly fitting capped horse teeth. Les sashays in wearing his designer cape, signature (Le)Corbu(sier) glasses, bow tie, tasseled suede loafers and air of arrogance. Not to be outdone, Sy brings along his air of arrogance. There actually might not be enough oxygen in the room to sustain both. Les carries a series of 'designers' pens to draw on the paper covering the dining table.

Sy: "Great to finally meet you Les. Seems like you're the flavor of the day."

Les smirkly grins thinking: 'I ccccertainly am."

Les says "Only the best developers use me."

Sy: "Now you can count me in that group - I've got a piece of land and want to build 10,000 condo apartments that I can sell at $7,000 a square foot. With all that foreign money flowing into the US, the demand is so fuckin hot, I can't miss! Hey – did you know that the baseball player Babe Ruth was called the 'Sultan of Swat'? Well I've got a famous athlete who calls himself the 'Sultan of Twat' and will buy five floors at $20 mil a piece. Make it a mix of 3, 4 and 5 bedrooms, etc. - you probably already know the formula layouts. **Les – I want a fuckin masterpiece building**."

Les: "Sy – I like a man with ambition. Do you have a budget?"

Sy side steps the question and continues, very animated.

"**Les – I want the Taj Mahal of residential buildings. I want to change the skyline. I want my building so prominent; it's a goddamn beacon for ocean-going**

ships to use as a navigational guide. So fuckin' tall it'll cast a shadow on South America. I want to change the center of gravity of the earth. I want it to be the 9th wonder of the world. DOYOUHEARME!!! I want my name emblazoned on the front page of all the newspapers– so every other shmuck developing buildings is jealous.

I think there's a fuckin spot for me at Mount Rushmore - next to George, Tom, Abe and Teddy. Les – DOYOUGETME?"

Les has heard this type of hubris before from other developers and he's also heard news reports from many of the angry tenants in buildings he owns and the questionable ethics of Sy Phillis –where he's turned off heat during the winter, where's no lighting in the hallways, broken plumbing pipes, rats, roaches and other vermin abound, stiffing contractors, not paying his bills, lawsuits, liens, stop work orders, building code compliance issues, and court ordered injunctions, just to name a few.

Les: "Sy – I will develop a ccconccept that'll make you soooooo excited, you'll have perpetual priapism – and won't you be lucky."

Sy doesn't know what priapism means – but pretends to, grinning ear to ear.

Sy: "Yeh, Yeh – tell me more."

Les: "I'm ssein' dtis building . . . . ." and he starts to sketch on the paper table covering. He draws a very, very, very tall building covering the length of the table and dots in a tiny streetscape entourage. To enhance the drama of scale, Les sketches the Empire State Building, which amounts to 1/64th the height of the ginormous tower that covers the entire length of the table. Sy has never seen anything like this and is so excited, he starts to shake and quiver. He reaches into to his pocket to grab a handful of Xanax.

"Yeh baby c'mon … Yeh…" as if he's at the track watching his 200 – 1 odds filly finish first.

Les: **"**Sy –lisssten to me."

With great puffery, pedigree nostrils flaring and with his slight lisp, he says: "I'm a cconceptualist and areteest. I will idealize an overly spectacular edifice for you but after I develop the design concept, you'll have to find another architect to take it on. I can't be bothered with construction documents or the minutia of details, etc. etc., which I find terribly 'boorrrhing' and then to boot, dealing with the mediocrity of sub consultants-– EECCHH! I find the building code completely restrictive, constraining and have no patience with the miscreants at the building department. And if you expect me to review shop drawings - **FORGET IT**!"

Sy gets momentarily distracted as a young buxom waitress walks by and he fiddles with his 40 year old marriage band thinking . . . 'Boy, could I use a nooner' and raises his eyebrows to such an extent, his hairpiece shifts and his facial make-up cracks. With that, Sy says to Les:

"Let's get started. Where do we go from here?"

Les: "I'll send you a proposal for design concept work – only."

Sy is now faced with finding another architect to complete what the Starchitect will not. The role of this other architect is to be the architect of record or AOR. The AOR takes the conceptual idea and makes it work on 'paper' while at the same time coordinating and interfacing with all other consultants required on a new residential building.

The AOR's work is done with little or marginal credit at the end. Sy has heard that Borborygmi (*def. the grumbling sound your stomach makes when you are hungry*) Architects (BA) (who are always starving for work) and Keister Kisser Architects (KKA) have both acted as AORs on other residential projects. He checks out the two firms' websites and sees that each profile a number of residential buildings. Actually, other than the name and location of each building, the buildings are all pretty much the same. Quite interestingly each building's got a name as if to enhance its presence. Even very non-descript residential buildings have names such as 'The Bush' or 'The Why' which might just slightly elevate its stature as follows: In casual conversations, it's frequently asked:

"So where do you live?"

The respondent: "I live at The Why."

The questioner would be impressed. Public buildings certainly deserve a name. I'm not so sure that residential buildings – unless architecturally unique – do.

Historically, an architect would responsibly take a project on and see it completely through to fruition. Not so in this case. Now with the advent of the Starchitect, even those unlicensed to practice architecture are designing buildings teaming up with a licensed architect who becomes the AOR. Bear in mind that among AORs, there are many very talented architects who haven't had the good fortune to be recognized as very competent designers – certainly, as competent as any Starchitect – simply because they haven't had the press or spent money on public relations coverage.

Sy decides to first call Keister Kisser Architects (KKA) and inquire about taking on the role of AOR. It's important to note the mindset of the developer. Other than the exorbitant fees he's reluctantly agreed to pay to the Starchitect, he's got to buy the AOR services at the lowest possible cost – irrespective of what the AOR contributes.

So the following is what might occur when the developer proceeds with trying to 'negotiate low fees':

Phone rings at Keister Kisser Architects.

Receptionist: "Good morning, Keister Kisser Architects, Moaner Fordic speaking, how may I direct your call?"

Caller: "Please hold for Mr. Philis" and the same nonsense about holding on occurs but Moaner endures. Finally, with a commanding voice:

"This is Sy Philis. Do you know who I am? I want to speak with one of the principals of Keister Kisser Architects about a new project."

Moaner: "Please hold – I'll get Mr. Kisser on the line."

"Woody Kisser here; who do I have the pleasure of speaking with?"

Again in a commanding voice:

"This is Sy Philis. Do you know who I am?"

Woody thinks he's heard of him but not sure in what context and becomes a little defensive. Sy starts firing a barrage of questions:

"HaveyoudesignedanyresidentialbuildingsImight beawareof? Whatdevelopershaveyouworkedforprev iously? DoyouknowLesIsmore-the famousstarchitect? Leswill bedesigninganextraordinaryresidentialbuild ing forme! I'mlookingforanarchitectofrecordtowo rkwithLes! What's yourfee!!!? Howmuchinsurancedo youcarry? Howlargeisyourstaff!!!!!?"

'*How large is my staff*? Woody thinks to himself: 'what is he really getting at?' as he fantasizes about his receptionist, Moaner. **"What! What!? What!?"**

Then Sy (with his bottom fishing mindset) calls Borborygmi (*def. the grumbling sound that emanates from an empty stomach*) Architects (BA) and fires off the same aggressive questions trying to get the lowest fee for the role of the AOR**.** Borborygmi Architects are always hungry for work.

Following the call, Sy requests proposals from KKA and BA to be the AOR and both firms return fees that are almost identical and quite reasonable. Sy first calls KKA whereby Moaner passes the call on to Woody Kisser. Then the following ensues:

"Woody Kisser here, how can I help you?"

Sy: "I received your proposal to be the architect of record. **Areyou fuckingserious? It'sgoddamntwicewhatI gotfromanotherarchitect. Do youwantthisproject?"** Woody's, somewhat stunned, replies: "Yes, of course we do, Mr. Philis."

Sy: **"Wellifyoudo,youbettertakeafuckin'hat chettoyourfuckin'fees!"** and slams the phone down. Sy then calls BA and hears a tiny breathy voice:

"Good Morning, Borborygmi Architects, Taint speaking, may I ax who's calling?"

Sy: "Hello? Hello? I can't hear you!"

"This is Taint, may I ax who's calling?"

Sy's thinking – I must be going fuckin' deaf! as he mouths a handful of antacids:

"I want to talk to Shelia Duyea. Iis she in? She sent me a proposal for architectural fees."

Taint: "Just one moment. I'll ax if she's available."

Sy's wondering if she's a carpet muncher and waits impatiently.

"Shelia here – who do I have the pleasure of speaking with?"

Sy's tone now turns somewhat less abrasive.

Sy: "Shelia, this is Sy Philis. You responded to my request for a fee to be the architect of record on my fantabulous new condo I'm building with the famous Starchitect Les Ismore. **Yourfeeismorethantwoandahalftimesthefeelg otfromanotherarchitect.Do youwantthisproject?"**

Shelia: "Yes we most certainly do."

Sy: "Ms. Duyea, listen to me. **Ineedyoutotakeanother veryhardlookat yourfee.I'mtalkingabouttakinadamn chainsawtoyourfee,get it?** That's of course if you want the job. And get back to me posthaste, *comprende*?"

He summarily hangs up.

Shelia's somewhat taken aback. Both firms resubmit revised fees and Sy continues to pit one against another up to the point where he finally decides on the firm who submitted the lowest fee; Keister Kisser. The conversation between Sy and Keister Kisser then goes like this:

"Kisser – this is Sy Philis. I got your revised fee. Knock off 15% and it's yours."

Woody reluctantly agrees thinking 'A bird in the hand…'

Sy now arranges for a 10:00 am meeting with Les and Woody at Les's office. Everyone agrees to the time. Woody arrives at Ismore Architects' office at 10:00 sharp and announces himself to Framunda, who's at the front desk. She hands him a sanitary hand wipe and says:

"Mr. Ismore will be with you when he finishes his business with China."

Woody's thinking 'What's with the sanitary wipe?' as he sits down on one of the designer chairs and waits and waits and waits. Forty-five minutes pass but there's no sign of Sy Phillis or any word from Framunda about Les. Woody starts hearing some strange moans, groans and pounding coming from a locked office. Moments later, he sees a young Asian boy leaving the locked office pulling his pants up, holding his backside and quickly exiting towards the elevator.

Framunda says: "Mr. Ismore is now finished with his China business and will be with you momentarily."

Woody's thoroughly confused as Sy now breezes in and says:

"Fraumunda, I'll have my usual. Kisser – how'a doin? Let's go" and marches right into the open conference room.

"Tell Les I want to start *now!*"

Les walks in barefooted, adjusting the zipper on his slacks.

Sy: "Les – meet Kisser – what's your first name again – I forgot?"

"Woody."

Les likes Woody's name. "It's Woody."

Sy: "So Les – show us your fantabulous design," whereupon Les uncoils a roll of sketch paper along the entire length of the eight foot conference table, unveiling an edifice of unimaginable height. Sy starts to salivate and his eyes bulge as do his suit trousers. Woody is slack jawed.

Les: "Dtisss beauty is six hundred stories of sumptuous, orgasmic elegance."

Sy's so excited, he's dripping. Woody's thinking: 'What the hell did I get myself into?'

Les: "Boys and Girls; you'll be able to see the Kremlin from the penthouse."

Sy's so excited; he breaks an ampoule of smelling salts. Les then shows a sketch example of a three apartment floor layout.

Woody's thinking: "This guy's a fricken idiot; he has two elevators serving 10,000 apartments, no structural system, missing shaft space, exit stairs that don't meet the building code and on and on. He decides to speak up:

"Les, I, ah, noticed that there's no structure system in your layout, the exit stairs don't meet code and just two elevators serving, uh, . . ."

Les summarily interrupts:

"Sy, the deliciousness of the paisley wall covering plus the Mongolian veneer will bring out the flesh tones of the residents" and turns to Woody, with a pitched voice of scorn and raised eyebrows:

"Voudy – I will not allow moy 'kreatesuns' to be in any way hindered with such silly or mundane details. I'm sure you'll work out all of your isshues."

Woody's thinking a good name for Sy's building would be **'Shock and Awe.'** Meanwhile, Sy, with a continued experience of proptosis, trousers now stained, can't believe what he's seeing and hugs Les saying:

"Wow! You've done it!"

Woody's thinking: 'Maybe I should apply for a cab driver's license' while there's a loud quiet in the room, accompanying the study of Les's design when Woody asks:

"Les, what type of heating and air conditioning system do you envision?"

Les, nostrils again flaring, arched eyebrows pitched, staring him down, arrogantly responds:

"Vood - would you ask Picasso what type of frame he wants around his art? Please – let's not be childish."

Woody's now wondering if he can support his family operating a food cart. Sy then turns to Woody and asks the proverbial demanding question:

"Woody – how quickly can I get a building permit?"

Woody's between a rock and a hard place. He needs the work but does he need the headache? So Woody heads back to his office and meets with his associate Constant Weiner. Constant is always negative, wears her smile button upside down, makes a point of drinking less than half a glass of water as a statement of her demeanor and also suffers from the debilitating condition of Ocular Rectumitis. As a matter of note, health scientists have been studying this pathogen for years and have yet to find a cure. A brief synopsis from a medical expert is as follows:

> *"Ocular rectumitis is a serious condition where the rectum and eyeballs are connected through the nervous system. In this condition, nervous system signals are transmitted to the brain which results in 'a shitty outlook on life'."*

Woody tries to put a positive spin on the conversation that goes as follows:

"Constant– I just had a meeting with Sy Philis the developer and Les Ismore - the 'Starchitect' to kick off a new project."

Constant, projecting discontent, frowns, hoping Woody would return with a project to design homeless shelters. Constant:

"Woody – why would you want to work for such developer reprobates – when we should be aspiring to design projects for the needy?"

Woody thinks to himself: 'Last time I worked on a housing project, I got assaulted, raped, my car was covered in graffiti, vandalized and someone took a dump on my hood.' He politely responds:

"Constant; we have a chance to make some money and work on a high profile project. We can't money working on community housing. Now we have a chance to work for Sy Philis."

Constant remembers that Sy Philis was once charged with infecting a state official for relief he received on a land deal and also cited for the unauthorized demolition of an occupied building at night without a permit where people were killed. Constant, in a deep loud voice exclaims:

"Well, I better get a penicillin vaccine, when does the project kick off?"

Woody: "Now!"

Constant retorts: "Well, what about the PTO (*def: Paid Time Off*) -- I have?"

"What?!" Woody responds. "You can't take time off now. Please, postpone it."

Constant: "I planned and have already paid for the trip for my sex change operation. If I don't go, will you reimburse me for all my expenses and pay me significantly extra for time I spend working here?"

Woody, to himself: 'I just can't win- ah fuck it."

Just then the phone rings and Moaner announces:

"Woody; it's Sy Philis."

Sy: "Woody – **Iwantthosefuckin'plansfastandwantyoutofuckin'self-certifythemsoIcangetafuckin'buildingpermit – gotme?**"

'Self-certify a new building? No fricken way!' Woody thinks as he now has to produce construction documents and also coordinate with the team of sub-consultants hired by Philis. As a side note, Philis, to save money, has selected a mix of questionable consultants. The only commonality is that not one speaks English, all need interpreters and rely on local engineers to become their Engineer of Record. Philis has also contracted STD to act as the Construction Manager (CM).

'Ah shit' Woody thinks as he steps out for a break, stops off at a local corner hot dog stand and orders a 'fully loaded tube steak' whereby he asks the vendor, how much money he takes home from his business endeavor. The vendor, responding in broken English quizzically responds:

"300 cash money per yeek."

Woody's thinks: 'If I moved my family to a trailer park, I might be able to swing that.' However, Woody's trying to be optimistic, so he confers with Constant and decides to call the first meeting with the sub-consultants and invites Les.

Les responds: "Vood –woy in gods'heavens name vood I want to attend a meeting with a group completely below my social caliber which will be predictably banal? You figure it out. I need time to spend exploring my creativity and must now leave to meditate and get acupuncture."

Woody mumbles to himself: 'This guy's a damn turd. I think the last building he designed was referred to as the Pig with Lipstick.'

So the first meeting is scheduled for 11:00 am at Woody's office. Consultants are suggested to bring their lunch. Each shows up in their native garb along with their interpreters. The mechanical engineer brings a Sterno stove and starts cooking rhinoceros with sauerkraut, the plumbing engineer's brought buffalo scrotum and the conference room smells really bad. Constant's wearing a gas mask and sprays the room with disinfectant. The acoustical ceiling tiles start to buckle from the food stench. Woody explains the project which in turn gets translated to the group and rolls out the elevation of the building. The shear verticality has everyone completely awestruck. The structural engineer balances a chopstick vertically on the table and makes strange deep grunting sounds then pronounces "石头 !!!" (Holy shit!!!) He's wondering what computer program is available that has enough R.A.M. to calculate and determine what counteracting forces that will be imposed on the structure. He by-passes his interpreter and asks:

"OOdy – thimk maba youa needa meteorologist for wond currents. Suddenly and surprisingly, Les saunters in and pronounces:

"What are you doing to my baby?" and then screams out: "WHAT IN GOD'S NAME IS THAT STINK!?" and faints. There's suddenly a lot of commotion. Moaner comes running into the room, kneels and bends over Les. Woody's standing behind her and notices the string of her tiny thong revealed by her form fitting jeans sliding down her butt. Woody's got to be very careful with sexual harassment lawsuits so prevalent today, however he's walked on the razors edge before and what will be – well you know.

The mechanical engineer clearly doesn't understand the code requirements for a residential building. When Woody asks about what heating and cooling system he recommends, the engineer suggests adding kerosene candles and light bulbs for heating and ceiling fans for cooling. Woody's head collapses from frustration but in the spirit of 'leading the charge,' he's not giving up, and asks for an alternate. The engineer responds:

"Mon, I dink ah ferepit for hea-**TING** - work; water soaked muslin for cool – work."

Woody then asks the structural engineer what computer program he uses at which point the engineer pulls out an abacus from his brief case. Woody starting to boil, walks out of the conference room and calls Sy Philis. He gets a recording:

"Office of Sy Philis ; *'This call may be monitored for quality assurance and training purposes. Press 1 for English; 2 for Spanish; 3 for Russian; 4 for Chinese; 5 for Tagalog; 6 for German; 7 for Italian; 8 Sindhi; 9 for Latvian,* etc. etc. etc."

'Quality and training purposes – who's he fooling?'

Woody's losing it and finally, after hearing a monotone selection of over 100 languages, starts pounding on 0 hoping to get an operator when he finally hears:

"Scheleze speaking - how can I help you?"

Frustrated, Woody yells out: **"I WANT TO TALK TO SY PHILISRIGHT NOW!"**

Scheleze: "Well –don't scream at me. Mr. Philis is on a conference call. Shall I take a message and have him call you back or . . ."

Woody interrupts: "I'll hold. And I don't give a shit how long I have to wait." And then wait he does. All of a sudden, he hears a dial tone. 'What the fuck is that?'

He calls again and gets the same recording.

'Press 1 for English; 2 for Spanish; 3 for Russian; 4 for Chinese;' and so on. Incensed, Woody decides to go over

to Sy's office. At the elevator lobby of Sy's building, he is confronted by a menacing looking armed security guard. The guard looks like a former sumo wrestler who lost a fight with a gorilla. He's got a patch over one eye, large flattened nose, a major gash scar across his face, neck larger than his head and missing every other tooth.

"Hooa here ta see?" says he in a booming voice as he stands over Woody, staring down at him.

"I'm here to see Sy Philis."

"He ain't in" replies the guard.

Woody glances at the wall directory and sees Sy Philis's name and floor designations with twenty different associated corporations. The guard temporarily gets distracted by a huge delivery of boxes and Woody scurries to the elevator. He exits onto Sy's floor. The waiting area is completely bare - no chairs, couches or anything, just a lot of security cameras and an intercom. Woody activates the intercom button. He hears the crackling voice of Scheleze.

"Can oi help you?"

Woody: "I've got to speak to Sy Philis."

Scheleze: "He's on a conference call."

"BULLLSHIT, DON'T GIVE ME THAT DAMN CRAP." Woody screams. **"HE'S ALWAYS ON A GOD DAMN CONFERENCE CALL – HE'S DUCKING ME."**

Woody then takes his fist and starts banging on the door.

"I WANT TO SEE PHILIS -NOW!"

Scheleze, through the intercom: "You'll have to wait for Mr. Philis to become available."

Two hours later, Scheleze opens the heavily reinforced entrance door and sees Woody lying on his back on the floor.

Scheleze: "Mr. Philis will see you now" and then she escorts Woody through a cluttered labyrinth of overstuffed banker boxes, piles of files and paper and pictures of Philis shaking hands with notorious political dignitaries – most now in prision - hanging on the walls. Woody enters Sy's small and very messy office. Sy stands up and says:

"Look, you little fuckin' monkey, what gives you the right to think you can just barge in here like this?"

Woody's a little taken aback by Sy's aggressive posture.

"And let me tell you something else; I selected you over another architect who had a much, much, much lower fee and better credentials. Don't let me regret picking you. Now what's your fuckin beef?"

Woody, stunned and at a loss for words, takes a deep breath and says:

"Mr. Philis – the consultants you picked for this project -- well I, uh, mean, uh the engineer uses an abacus and I uh . . ."

Sy interrupts. "Look - I only pick the crème de la crème. You're a snail darter in my book and should be grateful you're even working with great engineering minds. Stop being a fuckin whus and get me those permit drawings. We've got a contract. And by the way, I called Busta Pustule Yurchin of STD. I've contracted with him and he'll be contacting you so get back to your office and *deliver.*"

Woody's heard of STD and their reputation and the way they've impacted others. Yurchin's been convicted twice of extortion and racketeering and sentenced but got off both times on technicalities.

Deliver? Woody's wondering if he's about to become an additive to a concrete mix. Woody goes back to his office and starts reading his contract with Philis. In his haste to sign it, he overlooked numerous paragraphs for liquidated damages and recourse based on a delivery date certain amongst other onerous obligations.

'Shit' I'm in a fucking bind!'

Philis's one-sided contract has no provisions for 'either party termination' and the guarantee clauses as written would render Woody's professional liability insurance coverage null and void. He's flying 'bareback.' For advice, Woody reaches out to Chase Mee, a well-known building department expeditor. Chase has a lot of people in the building department in his back pocket who have granted him special considerations on his interpretations of the building code. His license has been suspended and reinstated numerous times. Chase uses a non-traceable cell phone, has no office, no e-mail address and only takes cash up front. He has specific protocols when one wants to meet with him – specifically the location, which is always changing. Chase and Woody finally meet at a distant corner table in an obscure coffee shop. Chase is wearing mirrored sunglasses.

Woody: "Chase – I'm in fucking bind. I signed on as the architect of record for Sy Philis and just realized there are provisions in the contract that are uninsurable and furthermore have due dates.

Chase interrupts: "Why I should help you? You no pay me last time. You talk me like me fool. Now you work for Sy Philis – man like bad disease. Now you fool."

Woody drops his head in his hands.

Chase continues: "Old Chinese proverb: 'Man who turn back on mirror, bend over and look back between legs see asshole.' Woody – you asshole for working for Philis. Building Department no like him. Too many problems."

Woody: "Chase, please! I apologize. The billing issue was an oversight and we weren't paid by our client."

Chase: "Why you make you problem mine?"

Woody: "Chase; I need your help. I've got to a limited amount of time to get him a building permit. Please!"

Chase: "How Moaner?"

Woody: "She's swell. Ask her out. Another thing, Philis contracted STD as the Construction Manager."

Chase looks over his sunglasses and says: "Old Chinese proverb: 'Man who turn back on mirror second time, bend over and look back between legs see bloody asshole!' STD bad news."

Woody says to Chase: "Look, I really need your help."

Chase, thinking about it, twirls his moustache and says: "Okay. $50 gees for permit help. You know how I work."

Woody's eyes roll - $50 thou - yikes. He's got to figure a way to get $50,000 in cash and goes back to his office. On the way, he's thinking of different possibilities to get this money, knowing that Chase will 'come through' if he does. Arriving at his office, Moaner, looking particularly provocative today, tells Woody there's a 'gentleman of sort' waiting for him in the conference room. Woody walks in.

"How'a doin? I'm Busta Urchin from STD. Hey buddy – you got some hot-looking babe with some major headlights on high beam out there."

Woody: "Yeah, I know. Why are you here?"

Busta responds: "Sy Philis told me to look over your shoulder. He's feeling lots of pressure and wants to get in the ground."

Woody thinks I wish Philis was already 'in the ground.' Woody then asks Constant to join the meeting. Constant walks in and is introduced to Busta. Immediately sparks start to fly.

Busta, staring at her upper lip, comments:

"Shoulda brung a razor; heh heh."

Constant replies: "What are you referring to?" staring back at him.

Busta responds: "Da drahins – relax - I'm here to help the process. Hey - what type a name is Constant? Like constant pain in the ass - heh heh?"

Constant doesn't like his type, particularly the tattooed knuckles spelling out <u>F</u> <u>U</u> <u>C</u> <u>K</u> <u>L</u> <u>O</u> <u>V</u> <u>E</u> along with his skinhead view of personal freedoms.

Woody jumps in and tries to quickly defray the tension.

"Hey, guys; cool it!" he exclaims. "We've only got six weeks to get a filing set into the building department."

Busta pipes in: "No sweat! I'll give you a set of 'drahins' from another project. Just cut the title block off, add yours, change a few things and you'll be ready to roll. Dem jerk-offs at the buildings department won't know any better."

Woody: "Busta; do you know Chase Mee the expeditor?"

Busta replies: "Yeah, I know of him. Everyone knows him. That chink gets shit approved! He's got pictures – and I don't know how he got 'em – of a few commissioners and examiners getting blow jobs across the street at The Head, a bar downtown frequented by city workers at lunchtime. I even seen him convince an inspector that a '20 story seement buildin' needed only one means of exit. Mee told 'em there'd be so few livin' in da bildin,' the likelyhood of a people tryin' to get out in case of a fire didn't exist. And what about that commissioner who got caught for doin' crack in his office – who do you think supplied him? Fuckin' Mee."

Woody's thinking about Busta's offer of using someone else's drawings and incorporating them into his set. Busta gets up and hands him his business card and leaves. Woody looks at the card. Behind the STD logo is a lenticular pattern showing a bikini clad woman who becomes naked when the plane of the card is turned. When Constant sees it, she frowns then sits with Woody to discuss a strategy for producing the documents. Woody's feeling lots of pressure to meet the deadline, and acutely aware of Philis's well-known proclivities to sue. They discuss Busta's idea of using documents prepared by others and decide to order lunch. When lunch arrives, it comes with the latest edition of the local tabloid with the headlines:

'DEVELOPER UNDER INVESTIGATION FOR RECYCLING UNTREATED SEWAGE FOR DRINKING WATER.'

'Well known city slum lord accused of using toilet flushings for drinking water in low income housing to save money on water bills.'

And there is a picture of Sy Philis with his dirt bag attorney completely denying the charges. Both Constant and Woody can't finish their lunches. Moaner brings in a certified letter. Woody's thinking 'Oh shit.' The letter is from Schnoz & Snot Attorneys LLC. and reads as follows:

'Pursuant to the Agreement between Tower Xcellance Partners Ltd. and Kesiter Kisser Architects, please note that a full and valid building permit must be ready for a contractor to commence work for the referenced project no later than 42 calendar days from the date of this letter.

Failure to achieve this will result in full and extensive damages sought by Tower Xcellance Partners Ltd.'

Woody leaves the conference room and sees a bouquet of flowers and box of chocolate on Moaner's desk. He also notices a card with some scribbling on it. Moaner's not at her desk so he takes a peak at the note. *You're amazing – I feel like a million dollars – much love – SP.*

Woody's confused. He thought Moaner already had a boyfriend. Who's SP? Could it be Sy Philis? Could he be cavorting with his secretary? Woody's heard – second hand of course – that Moaner's a man-eater. She knows how to use her 'money maker' to get what she wants. However, Woody needs money and he certainly doesn't have a 'money maker.' He's got payroll, rent, and numerous expenses and he has to come up with $50,000 in cash for the expeditor.

He calls Sy Philis's office. After listening to the frustrating selection of language choices, he finally gets Scheleze on the phone and inquires about past due invoices that are very late. Scheleze says they already mailed his checks – weeks ago. Woody asks for duplicates. Scheleze says he'll have to wait since the checks might arrive any day. (The checks were never mailed which is standard operating procedure for Philis).

Woody's in a bind. He's got money pressures and reaches out to Busta who knows someone who knows someone, etc. He gets the name of Gonif Geltmore who loans money out at a 25% vig. He knows of another 'lender,' Rep Tilian. Tilian's a familiar name associated with the construction industry. Tilian's got a cold hearted reputation. Woody's starting to get heart palpitations and having a hard time breathing. Actually he's having a panic attack. Where's he going to get his money? Woody confers with Constant.

"Constant, I know how you feel about working with Busta, but I think we need him as an ally. I'm feeling extraordinary pressure to produce the construction documents within the time frame. And we've only got $20 in the bank. We're in a major cash crunch."

Constant responds:

"What about a loan? Can we get out of this project?"

Woody: "Loan – against what? I've got no collateral and **NO** – I can't get out of this project since there's a non-revocable binding clause and other bullshit in the contract."

Constant: "What? Why did you ever stupidly agree to that?"

Woody:" I overlooked that and other aspects of the one sided contract, including the delivery date because I was so anxious to get the project. I'm screwed."

Constant: "You might say that and more. If you can get Busta to stop with his antifeminists comments, I might be able to work with him, begrudgingly."

Meanwhile, Paine Carbuncle, a tenant in one of Philis's other development projects that's been in the news for lack of heat and running water along with a rat infestation has assembled an angry group to protest the development of Philis's new project. Unfortunately, the only address they have is in front of Keister Kisser's office where hoards have gathered chanting:

"ONE, TWO, THREE, FOUR; WE DON'T WANT (Sy)Philis NO MORE!" Handmade signs and placards galore. Woody goes over to the window and sees the yelling throngs outside.

'What the hell?' Why are they targeting me?'

All of a sudden, a giant 40 foot high inflatable rat is in front of the entrance of Keister Kisser's office. Woody decides to go outside and confront them. As he emerges, the boos and chanting gets louder. Carbuncle picks up a bull horn:

"You ah da'grace Mitta Philis."

Then someone in the crowd tosses a loaded baby diaper which hits Woody in the face. Woody's so horrified and disgusted that he's about to blow lunch and then he screams back:

"I'm not Sy Philis. You've got the wrong office address. I'm just the architect."

Carbuncle responds: "You archie-o- tek? - den you guilty too for working for da' honky. Our bildins' ain't got no heat and da tap wata's shit brown. Why you design dis way?"

Woody yells back: **"I didn't design those buildings for Sy Philis – someone else did."**

"Where he at?" screams an inflamed Carbuncle.

"I don't know!" Woody screams back and hesitates, wondering if he should give out Philis's address.

Then Woody makes the following mistake yelling out:

"I'm going to call the cops if you don't disbandon!!!!" not realizing he's throwing gasoline on a fire to extinguish the furor.

"Tat'll be just fine since we brung some barbecue sauce to baste da' pigs in" screams back Carbuncle.

'Oh brother' thinks Woody - that just made things worse as the crowd is now embroiled. Woody, shielding his head, runs back inside just as another loaded used diaper splatters up against the building's entrance door. He returns to his office. Busta shows up with a large roll of drawings, brings Moaner a single rose and walks right into Keister Kisser's conference room. Moaner enters:

"Thank youoooooooooooo sooooooooo much, kiss, kiss, kiss, for the beautiful rose Mr. Urchin. Can I offer you anything?"

Moaner's dressed more provocatively than usual this day with her tight fitting outfit revealing her ample figure. The temperature in the conference room is so cold that her thimbled nipples just might break through her sheer brassiere. Busta obviously takes great notice and not a shy man, just comes out with it:

"What you can offer me, darlin', is a date."

"Oh Mr. Urchin; I'm so flattered."

Busta chimes in: "Please call me Busta."

"However, I'm sort of already involved."

Busta's sensing Moaner's hot and freewheeling motor, so he keeps coming.

"So what? I say we go out and have a great time. I say 'Let's paaarttay!!!"

Moaner already knows Busta's type so she'll just play him. Cooing, she says:

"***Bus***-turrr; I've heard you're quite the man with the right tool. I have a problem that you might be able to help me with."

Busta's splitting his shorts. "What is it honey?" he says pantingly.

"The closet door in my apartment is always coming off the track. Can you fix something like that?"

"Absolutely! When can I come over?"

Busta's thinking: 'Man, this is a slam dunk.'

But it ain't gonna happen, no how, no way. Moaner's just way too cool and savvy and so experienced, she can 'peg an oncoming freight train, blasting down the tracks many miles away.' So the next morning, Busta gets up, takes a very long shower, double scrubbing his privates, making sure they're ready for action. He douses himself with so much cheap cologne that the neighborhood dogs stop sniffing each other's ass and start pawing their snouts as he passes by on his way to Moaner's apartment.

At Moaner's front door, Busta's phone rings. It's Sy Philis.

"Urchin; where the fuck are you? Urchin!" he screams, **"where the fuck are you?"**

"I'm at Kisser's secretary's apartment – she axed me to fix sumptin." Phillis is now more incensed.

"You fucking idiot. What d'fuck are you doing there? Don't you listen to the news? I got a million screaming demonstrators in front of my building. They've got that inflated rat with a picture of me in his fuckin' mouth! Get your head out of your ass and get up there and take care of this; that's what I pay you for."

So, Urchin telephones 'Rocco -The Rodent Resolver' who runs a disreputable pest control business amongst other 'front' enterprises and explains the problem which 'The Resolver' handily deals with.

But back to Keister Kisser's office. Constant is pouring over the drawings Busta left behind. She says to Woody:

"I've got good news and bad news."

Woody: "Okay – give me the bad news first."

"It's the worst set of construction documents I've ever seen in my entire life. Whoever prepared them knows nothing about building construction, let alone the building code. You know the building that collapsed don't you – the contractor and the architect both went to jail?"

Woody: "Oh shit – then what possibly could be the good news?"

Constant: "It's the same set of consultants who Philis wants us to use on his project."

"Good Grief!!!!! That's Good News!???" exclaims Woody. Then Moaner hands Woody the day's mail. It's all bills – except for an official letter from the city. Hastily, Wood opens it:

Dear Responder:

On behalf of City department of Procurement Services, thank you for responding to the RFP requesting architectural services for a new Squatters Shelter. We received numerous very qualified submissions, making our selection decision very difficult. Unfortunately, your firm was not selected for this project. Try again next time.

Once again we thank you for your interest and response.

Please continue to access our website for new RFP opportunities and follows us on social media.

Have a nice day.
Fangool,

Woody has received this type of rejection letter many times before and he's getting immune.

'We just got a rejection notice from the city to design a Squatters Shelters.' Who the fuck are they kidding? What qualifications does one need to design a Squatters Shelter?

The way my career is going, I'll be squatting, somewhere, sometime. Woody's exhausted. He decides to go home much earlier than usual. "Poussey - I'm here" he exclaims as he opens the door to his apartment. Strangely, his wife's not there, though she usually is. Even stranger, the apartment's completely bare; totally empty. Woody opens the apartment door to check the corridor side numbered designation to see if he's in the right apartment. It's his apartment alright. Stunned doesn't come close to describing his state of mind. Woody's magnified sense of reality is now abstracted.

"What was I thinking when I married a kleptomaniac dominatrix with a gambling addiction?"

Seeking some level of sanity, he decides to go back to his office. Once there, he notices in the conference room, the silhouette of two in embrace. Now Woody's wondering if the oatmeal he had for breakfast was laced with LSD. A messenger drops off a letter from Poussey that reads as follows:

> *You piece of shit! It's all your fault. Because of you, I turned to gambling. Because of you, I got into S&M. Because of you, I developed IBS. Because of you, I crashed the car. Because of you, my hair's falling out. Because of you, I can't stop smoking. Because of you,it's raining. Because of you, my pants don't fit. Because of you, I'm always late. Because of you, my pen doesn't work.*

I sold all the furniture because you made me go into debt because of the gambling you forced me into and by the way, threw out your old stupid arcoteks drawings of some jerkoff named right, because they were stupid and ugly!!! Don't you ever try to contact me or your tattooed, pierced, blond and magenta haired daughter - you damn moron ! And so what if I like to whip and torture people – they like it and pay me for it –wimpster. MAN-UP!

Woody; by the way, honey, I was wondering, can you lend me some money until I get on my feet?

Poussey

Whew, thinks Woody, I can't believe I'm married to such a wonderful, sensitive, caring woman and have a multi-colored hair daughter with a body covered in tattoos.

Woody goes to his doctor and takes his annual physical. Everything is fine except for the on-going headaches he's been having which he attributes to stress. They are now getting almost unbearable. His doctor can't find anything and refers him to another doctor who refers him to another. All say that it's stress. Then he sees specialist after brain specialist. Takes test after test. Nothing.

Finally he sees a renowned expert - Dr. Thalamus, who very carefully and methodically studies Woody's multiple scans and charts. He calls Woody and tells him to get over to his office as soon as possible. Alarmed, Woody shows up.

"Mr. Kisser – do you believe in God?" the doctor asks.

"No - should I? Woody answers.

"Do you believe in eternal life in any form?"

"No – should I?"

The doctor then proceeds with:

"You're sitting across from me, looking me straight in the eye, breathing normally and very much alive, wondering why I'd be asking you these questions, correct? Please let me continue. If I said life was akin to an hour glass with sand running through it, would that make sense to you?"

"Yes" responds Woody.

"Okay. Can we then establish, for the sake of this conversation, that everyone's life is like an hour glass, with sand as a measure of time running through it, such that everyone's life has a different amount of sand in the upper portion of an hour glass – call it the future – correct? And that there are many variables and unknowns in every grain of sand yet to pass through the constriction point at the middle of the hour glass, which I call the present and the bottom portion the past which you can do nothing about. Does that make sense to you?"

"Yes. Are you a shrink?"

"No, I'm a neurosurgeon with expertise in brain pathologies."

"Then why the philosophical questions?" Woody inquires.

"Mr. Kisser – indulge me – please. I want you to think of each grain of sand as an aspect of time and fate. Just for the moment consider that there may be just a few small grains that have you leaving this office and getting hit by a bus – and then 'Puff!' Life as you know it is over – agreed – something you did not plan for?"

"I do - but that not a very pleasant thought" responds Woody.

"Exactly. My point is simple. Since you don't know what's in every grain of sand, it's important to live as if some of those small grains of sand have an agenda you might not be aware of."

"So?" Woody's now puzzled.

Doctor: "I'm going to give you something to relieve your headaches and I want you to venture forth fronting every issue of life – happy or not – savoring every instance. Take on every waking moment knowing there are small grains of sand that have an agenda – that may not in your best interest and conversely, small grains of sand that are specific to you with an agenda that is totally in your best interest."

"What's with all this philosophical nonsense, what are you talking about?" Woody asks.

"Mr. Kisser, you have, at best, nine months to live. You have an inoperable brain tumor, the type that metastasizes at a rate of one mm per week. Now I've made my point. Do you have any questions?"

"Whew!!!!! I'm speechless" Woody says.

"Actually you're not. Think about the moment 30 minutes ago when you walked into my office, completely unknowing about your brain tumor I just told you about; how are you any different, other than now knowing about my prognosis and that you are now concerned?

I am telling you to go and live your life while you have one. Take the medication I've prescribed; you'll have no headaches. From what you've told me about your life to date, it seems to me that you've assumed the role of a victim. I say 'Assume the role of a victor."

"Doctor, I have just one question. When you say I have maybe nine months to live, is there any hope I might live longer?"

"Mr. Kisser, you have an aggressive, inoperable cancer with a 100% mortality rate. However, with that said, the human body is quite amazing and so complex, that the greatest minds in medical science have yet to completely understand it all. So you ask me if there is hope and I say to you there's always hope. Maybe the odds are greatly stacked against you, but then in other nonrelated instances I have seen surprising and amazing reversals of fate. Please remember about those grains of sand and go out and live your life. There just might be a few grains within you that make you the exception to my diagnosis."

Woody leaves and goes to a local coffee shop to gather his thoughts. He decides not to get crazy about his predicaments. He wants to believe he's capable of being the victor. As far as his marriage to Poussey, he writes that off as a moment when he veered off the road of his life, knowing at the time, deep down, that she was toxic albeit exciting. So big deal! So he made a mistake. Let's move on.

Woody's got to be around positive energy; forget the negativity. Heading back to his office, he's thinking about his role as the AOR on the Philis project and all the hype created around the concept of a Starchitect. He just saw another article in the real estate section of the news:

> *'The Starchitect' Mo' Glass will design a new, even more than spectacular, residential condominium complex that will include a fitness center, spa, doggy day care, wife swapping amenities along with carpeted hallways and a new state of the art fire suppression system. The developer contends that this will be the first building where all occupants will save significant money by not watching reality television shows. Each occupant will be able to see and hear the 'action' of their neighbors through a gossamer wall system separating the apartments. The name of the new building will be called 'The Voyeur.'*

Unfortunately, 99% of all residential buildings are so formulaic, no wonder a developer has to use names the public is ostensibly impressed and familiar with in order to sell them. Woody's wondering how a name can become so credible without having credibility knowing 'If he builds it, they will come' one way or another.

In any event, Woody's now determined to finish Philis's project, irrespective of the constraints of time, consultants or personalities. He stops off at a local sporting goods shop and buys a sleeping bag, figuring that since he doesn't have a home to speak of anymore, he'll just camp out in his office and live there. Woody calls a meeting of all consultants and declares a 'state of urgency.'

'Report to my office tomorrow morning – 8:00 am sharp and be prepared to resolve all building systems.'

Woody's starting to get energized. Call this the resurrection of Woody.

All the consultants show up at 8:00 am and Woody's on a roll. He took the drawing set that Busta had dropped off and trashed it, incensed at the suggestion of using someone else's documents – thinking – what a 'fricken dirtbag' – I'm not going to deal with such an unethical asshole. Woody had taken Ismore's layouts and overnight, completely redrew them, adding all the proper exit stair towers, elevators, refining the apartments, and working out the structural, mechanical, electrical and plumbing systems, etc.

Constant arrives at the office.

"What's going on ?"

Woody responds:

"Constant, go take your vacation and stay on it permanently."

"Woody; what are you saying?"

"Constant, your non-stop bitching and complaining about the projects we have has gotten on my nerves. So leave and go work on homeless shelters and projects for the needy. It's a very admirable pursuit, but I don't have the stomach to deal with the bureaucracy with those who feed at the public trough. I do feel that there's an inequity in the design of that type of housing, however, the agencies who oversee it aren't interested in good design and unfortunately, some of the residents seem to tolerate graffiti, grime and crummy living standards which baffles me. I can run this show on my own. Good bye."

"You mean I'm fired?" she asks.

"You can use any verb you want, but I don't want you to be here anymore; I want you gone. Your negativity is too intolerable."

"Well fuck you – you jerk off!" she screams.

"Constant, you've got to do better than that. I've heard that type of language daily from my wife – soon to be my ex -- and I'm immune to it."

"Do I get severance pay?" she asks.

"What you get is severance – period – without the pay" he responds. Constant is now so pissed off, she takes her cup of half-filled water and throws it at Woody, missing by a mile. Woody's about to say something in response, but he refrains and then commands to the stunned consultants:

"PAST TENSE – BACK TO WORK!!!"

Constant storms out, slamming doors, cursing and yelling. Woody then explains the structural system he wants, the 4 pipe chilled water system with hot water boiler as part of the mechanical system, down to the heated floors and thermostatically controlled shower. Woody's figured everything out overnight. Standing at the end of the conference room table, he says:

"Gentlemen, I want you to take copies of my sketches, put them into working drawings and get them back to me for review in two weeks. No excuses. Any questions?"

The consultants are dumbfounded. Woody's on his 15th cup of coffee and very wired. The mechanical engineer asks:

"Mr. Voody – vy you nneda four pipes ven use ca usa one pipe – I no understand?"

Woody's now finished his 17th cup of coffee and vigorously trying to control his rapid firing mind.

'Oh shit! he's thinking.

"Listen to me and I'll explain the four pipe system." He takes out a sketch pad.

"Watch! You see - hot water from the boiler runs through one pipe and returns through the second pipe. Understand?"

"Uh-huh, I does."

"Okay; stay with me now. Chilled water runs through the third pipe and returns through the fourth pipe. Understand that?"

"Where chilled come from? Da bollar?"

"No, No!" and Woody takes a deep breath thinking 'Breathe in through your nose and out through your mouth' before going on: "It comes from the chille."

"What da chilla?" asks the engineer.

Totally frustrated, Woody says:

"I'll figure this myself, send it to you, and then just put it into computer aided drawings, okay"

"Yeh mon."

Then the structural engineer asks, as he fiddles with his abacus:

"Wuch you mean bundled tube?"

Woody's on his 25th cup of coffee by now. He should have 'mainlined' caffeine directly and carefully explains the concept.

"Ah so – no columns?"

Woody's thinking that Philis's selection of consultants is not going to 'cut it' so he'll have to 'ride the bull' himself. Very frustrated he asks the engineers as a group:

"Can you guys tell me where you received your education?"

The first to respond, who understood the question, answers:

"Mita Voody, I vent ta' da' school I seen on da' cover of da' matches."

'Breathe in through your nose, out through your mouth, again and again while you close your eyes and think about the grains of sand.'

Woody's a little twisted around and now snorting the coffee grounds. Actually, most residential condominium buildings have almost the same building systems, components and apartment layouts that Woody is more than familiar with. Hardly rocket science.

So as Woody's holding court with the beleaguered consultants, Busta shows up unannounced and walks right into the meeting. Woody responds accordingly: "Can I help you?"

"I'm here to check on the status of the project. Hey, where's Butch?" Busta asks, referring to Constant .

"She's gone as well as you're going to be."

"Hey, who the fuck do you think you're talking to, squirrel meat?"

Woody responds: "I'm talking to you, you god damn psychopath now get the hell out of my office."

"I've got chunks of guys like you in my shit, don't you fuck with me!"

The consultants sitting around are starting to duck for cover, they've never encountered anything like this.

Woody screams: "Now get the hell out of my office!"

Busta leaves and stops by Moaner's desk.

"Hey babe, sorry about the other day. I got a call from the boss, but you didn't respond when I er 'rung your bell."

"Oh? ***Bus-***turrr ! Ooh– did you ring my bell? I didn't notice. Maybe that needs to be fixed as well!"

Actually Moaner wasn't even home, but is acting like she was. Busta then says:

"What the hell is going on with your boss? He threw me out of the conference room?"

Moaner: "Oh ***Bus-***turrr! I heard about that; poor Woody's simply under a lot of pressure. He just fired Constant and I heard him mumbling that his wife left him."

So then Busta again inquires when can he come over to her apartment and Moaner responds:

"Oh ***Bus-***turrr! Anytime that's convenient for you that I can fit into my tight schedule."

Busta's popping buttons and boy would he like to fit into her tight schedule. All of a sudden, there's a call from Sy Phillis. He wants an update on the status of the drawings and permit filing. Woody picks up the phone, his eyes red and swollen, his eyebrows arched and his voice like Lucifier's:

"What?"

Complete silence on the other end.

"Please hold for Mr. Philis."

Woody hangs up. Phone rings a second time.

"Please hold for Mr. Philis."

Woody hangs up again. Phone rings a third time.

"Kisser, what the hell's going on?" yells Philis.

Woody hangs up again.

Now Sy's confused and Woody has Moaner call Philis. He hears one side of the conversation:

"Mr. Philis, it's Moaner Fordic from Keister Kisser Architects. Yes, thank you," Moaner starts to whisper, "Oh Sy . . . yes . . . prefer Italian . . . of course I'm wet when I talk to you."

Then she returns to a normal voice noticing Woody's listening .

"Mr. Philis, Woody asked me to call you. He's too busy to talk. He's deeply immersed in your project . . . yes Sy . . . 8:00. Thank you, Mr. Philis."

Woody's hip to what's going on between Moaner and Philis but he doesn't care. He's on a mission to complete and file the documents. Then Moaner tells him Chase Mee's on the phone.

"My brother! Whus up?" as Woody's got a bit of street jive levity in his voice.

"Kisser Wood,where my money at?" Mee asks.

Woody says: "Chase, I don't have a dime to my name to spend on expediting and have decided to file the drawing set myself."

Mee responds: "You fool Kisser! You get chopped up like suey at building department. You stay on line all day for nothing. You don't know how department work. You don't have any contacts. You wait and wait and wait like little lost boy at big bus terminal - no idea how to get to where to go. I know top inspectors. You don't have clue to way system works."

Woody responds: "I may not – but I'm going to learn."

"You learn?" Chase laughs. "You learn how to eat shit sandwich. Ha! No book teach you process. Need contacts. Department reviewer see novice, they make you turn on spit**."**

Woody's so tightly wired from free basing coffee grinds after consuming 30 cups of coffee that he just lets it fly:

"Chase, why don't you turn and split?? I don't have the ridiculous amount of money you're trying to extort from me. Don't like the idea of your contacts bending the review process because you have compromising pictures of them and quite frankly the 'old boys club' atmosphere, particularly paying off some of the reviewers for approvals as well as supplying them drugs is completely abhorrent to me. Please leave now!"

"Okay Kissa, you be sorry. Old Chinese Proverb ' Man who learn to shave on own face, get cut, bleed to death'."

Woody retorts: " Chase, I use an electric razor, so please leave now!"

Outside the conference room, Chase stops by Moaner's desk .

"What wrong him? You like Chinese food?" as he stares at her neck line. Just as Moaner's about to answer, the phone rings and it's a frantic call from Sy Philis.

"Moaner, I've got to speak to Woody right now, please."

Sy's tone is now very different as Woody picks up the phone:

"Woody, Sy Philis here, look I'm in a jam and need your help."

Woody says:

"How about paying your bills?"

"Is there a problem? I wasn't aware of it. I'll make sure you get your money ASAP, but in any event, I just received a rejection notice on a few zoning compliance applications that need your architect's seal. Just a small issue of course –no big deal - I'll send them over to you by messenger. Please take care of this. I need them back right away. I'll be forever grateful"

'Grateful? Bullshit' Woody thinks to himself.

Philis is a lying sack of shit. Like he's really not aware of my past due invoices; what a crock. Let's see when his money shows up. Later on as the day wears on, he sees Moaner returning from the ladies room where she has gotten all dolled up and changed into 'attention-getting attire.' Her dress is so short and skimpy, if she were to bend forward just 10 degrees while walking along traffic on a busy city street, it might cause a major vehicle pile-up. Woody, trying to restrain himself, can't help himself:

"Well, don't *you* look like a magazine item?"

Just then, Moaner's cell phone rings. Turning her back, she quickly answers in a whisper.

"Of course.... Honey....... I'll be down in a minute."

Woody's libido now gets the better of him, pumped with all that caffeine; his self-controlling systems are twisted askew:

"Hot date! Some lucky guy, eh? Wish it was me; Whew! You look great and smell good ; you're very hot" as he moves beyond her 'permissible' body space and places his arm around her shoulder. Moaner fires back:

"Woody! You're coming on to me. Maybe you should read your employment manual, particularly the section on sexual harassment."

As if Woody had been dunked into ice water, he quickly comes back to his senses.

"Moaner, I have no idea what you're talking about. I said what? What?"

Moaner's baffled as Woody maintains an air of total innocence.

"Woody; you said that I was very hot, and you commented on my perfume amongst other things. You came into my personal space and put your arm on me as well!"

Woody: "I did no such thing. You must be imagining it. I completely deny any of your accusations. I maintain only the highest moral and ethical standards in dealings with employees in my practice as well as my life. To assume otherwise is offensive. Moaner; do you believe life is like an hour glass filled with sand?"

Moaner's now completely confused.

"Are you making some weird reference to my wonderful figure, suggestively comparing it to an hour glass?"

"Do you think I'm comparing your figure to an hour glass? What are you talking about? I never noticed your figure" Woody counters, as Moaner's cell phone rings again, though this time her agitation is pronounced.

"Sy, relax; I'll be down in a minute!!"

Woody hears her and now thinks that in addition to being screwed by Philis, his secretary is too.

"So you're going out with Sy Philis; you know he's married?"

Moaner's still confused, and now frustrated and angry as well.

"Woody; do I pry into your life? Do I make suggestive sexual comments? Do I ask stupid questions about life being like sand? I don't need this crap, don't understand you and maybe I should sue you or speak to Busta and by the way, take a shower and shave for once. Since you've been living in this crummy office, even the cock roaches seem to like you."

Woody: "Moaner, you have choices and . . .

Moaner interrupts: "Damn straight I have choices! I quit. Get a life."

With that, she walks out of the office.

Woody thinks to himself: *'I just saved more payroll money; don't have to deal with her foolish career goal of becoming an actress; she just sits there all day reading the supermarket gazette; looking at herself in her makeup mirror; filing her nails while waiting to answer the phone that never rings and playing up to any guy she can get something from. Time will take its toll on her. Good riddance.'*

Woody's now on his own. No staff, no secretary. He's single-mindedly focused on finishing the construction documents for Sy's building. He's not going to cut any corners or job-out part of the project; he's just going to commit his whole existence to producing a quality set. He's even going to forego his favorite extracurricular activities including submarine race watching, playing Go; reading *Intelligencia* and pulling his pud. Woody's going to live like a monk. Day in day out; night after night; morning, noon and night. Woody presses on.

Time has become irrelevant. It's Woody's race against Sy's imposed deadline and the depleting grains of sand flowing through his hour glass. Just for a moment, he becomes introspective and ponders the driving motivational character of Christopher Columbus, Lewis and Clark and Pewee Herman. His determination is omnipotent. He has a single focus. Woody's pouring over every apartment layout, every detail, every wall section and every system making sure there are no redundancies, conflicts or busts. Drawings are scattered all over his conference room table and floor, thumb tacked up on walls, ceiling and scotch taped to windows. He's using a mobile intravenous feeding system filled with coffee and purchased a 4 foot 'doomsday wall clock.' He looks up from the table and sees Les Ismore standing in the conference room doorway.

Les: "Voody, vhat are you doing, pray tell?"

Woody, with his bloodshot eyes, stares back:

*"I'm re-designing the silly fantasy you sold Philis. I don't know how you got to where you are, **Mr. Starchitect**, but in*

my book, you are more of a decorator, not an architect, hyping to a certain breed of developer who could care less - less - hey that's your first fucking name isn't it - about providing creative and thoughtful living environments. Your blatant contempt for architectural protocols, building systems and life safety is abhorrent to me and . . ."

Les is stunned: "Voody, no one talks to me like this, you suud be 'assamed.' I've been published in the most fashionable glossy magazines, been the featured ssstory countless times in high end residential publications and received numerous requests to be on television. Look at you! This place is a Collyer brother's paradise. And *you* -- when was the last time *you* took a shower? I can smell your god awful breath and socks from where I'm ssstanding. Did someone make a poopy in your mouth? Is '*Z*' outhouse door open? Oh my gosh I might just faint! And what do you have, missstur, to show for your miserably sorry career?"

Woody, enflamed, responds: *"Ismore – you live in a world of total pretension, pretending to be above the sensibilities of others; pretending you have taste and pretending you're an architect. You don't know shit about how a building works. Just because you say you're an architect, doesn't give you license to promulgate all the hype you spread. All you care about is wall paper and paint. You're a sad commentary on the state of residential buildings."*

Ismore: "Well, I never in my life, er, ah . . .. I'll call Sy and you'll hear from him. I can't deal with anyone that upsets my karma." He walks out but turns back to Woody and says:

"Don't forget to put in the curtain rods."

Woody responds: "I think 'pudding *in'* the curtain rod is more in your scope and appropriate for you."

Ten minutes later Sy calls:

"Woody, what the hell are you doing to my team? You've got all the consultants running scared and now you've offended Les Ismore and by the way, where's that zoning application I need your seal on?"

Woody: "Sy, have you ever heard the expression: 'Some of the best projects are the ones you don't have?'"

Sy confused. "What are you talking about?"

Woody: "I stupidly signed on to this trip to hell, but nonetheless I did and am going to deliver what I agreed to. Have no worries Sy, you'll have your permit, and there's no need to try to intimidate me with letters from your lawyers – What was the firm's name? 'Booger and Booger,' or something like that. As for your zoning application, have Ismore put his seal on it"

Sy: "Woody,that will be a problem."

Woody: "Why?"

Sy: "Les doesn't have a license; he's an artist and creator of style."

Woody: "So he's not actually an architect?"

Sy: "Oh that's just a formality; don't belabor it. Architect, schmarchitect; Les has a much respected name among the upper class. He's always invited to the best cocktail parties where he schmoozes with actors, artists and benefactors."

Woody: "What? He's a prophet of hype. You have the same contemptuous regard for the architectural profession as does Ismore. Woody then imitates Les while saying: *'I kant be bothered with any sub consultants'* – "What type of b.s. is that? And look at the ridiculous consultants you've selected for this project. Do you know I'm completely redesigning the building so it works? And that includes all building systems. This crap about Les Ismore being a Starchitect is just bullshit! Where did that idea even come from? *'Gee, I guess a good P.R. firm.'* Sy, take your zoning problem somewhere else. By the way, I never received any money from you as you promised. You perpetuate one of the three greatest lies. I should take your project, roll it up and have you sit on the roll end, with grease supplied by your Starchitect."

Sy's now somewhat stuck. He needs his building permit otherwise his loan commitments will go south and it's too late to get another architect on board so he smartly decides to 'cool it' with Woody and says:

"You don't look well, smell sort of funky. I see you're hooked up to a mobile IV system and I notice your bloodshot eyes. Are you okay? By the way, I'd be honored if you attended my special event. Did you get an invitation?"

Woody: "Am I okay ? What does that mean, am I okay? And what event are you sponsoring?"

Sy:" I'm the chairman of *'The Non-For-Profit Ocular Rectumitis Foundation.'* My wife has that condition. Would you be so kind as to consider sponsoring an ad, it's only $25,000 for a quarter page and the who's who of the who's who will be there."

Woody thinks 'Shit, that's what Constant had and maybe his wife got that from living with Sy. He then says:

"Sy, say what?! You owe me money. I'm living on fucking fumes. How do you think I could pay for your supposed charity which is probably a sham?"

Sy: "I thought all architects were well-heeled."

Woody: **"Sy, just look at my feet. See those damn holes in my socks? They exist because I've worn through both the heels and soles of my shoes! I don't know any well-heeled architects, only high heeled Starchitects. Sy, I'm on one mission and that's to complete your project. Now hold on a minute, I have to fill up my IV bag. I think it's best I finish your project, file for a permit and leave the rest up to you and your cronies to build and that you and I not have any more conversations. Our chemistry doesn't mix well."**

Sy;

"Well if that's the way you feel, you won't be working on my next project."

Woody: **"Sy; your next project? I don't *want* your next project" and then** he hangs up.

Woody goes back to the conference room and starts to organize the set of construction documents, pouring over each sheet, checking, back checking and double checking for incongruities, duplications and redundancies. He wants to make this set 'air-tight.' Woody's also prepared the Specification Manual, which comprises part of the Construction Documents Set reading each relevant section and making sure everything applies and is consistent with the drawing set.

Woody's starting to feel a sense of accomplishment now that he's ahead of his doomsday clock. He calls all the sub-consultants and requires them to show up at his office the next morning with each engineer of record. They are to bring along their professional seals to affix and sign to the pertinent documents so that the set can be filed with the building department.

When the engineers arrive, they gather in the conference room where Woody has separated each respective discipline into piles. The structural engineer starts looking at his pile of drawings and first takes out his magnifying glass, then switches to high powered binoculars. He's never seen a 8,000 foot tall residential building or anything like this. He exclaims:

"石头" (Holy shit!)

Because of the height, the building's foundations are anchored to the core of the earth. The elevators are pressurized to a zero atmosphere environment, powered by Saturn propulsion jet engines and restrained by specially designed holding parachutes all within the core. The penthouse resident can reach their apartment from the ground floor within 6 seconds and at 11:00 pm watch the sunrise over the Kremlin. The building's sway, deflection and wind forces are transferred from the absorbing dampening devices into energy that activates the buildings pumps.

The mechanical engineer is amazed. The heating system takes advantage of the earth's hot core; the cooling system uses 55 degree water from the stream table below the earth's surface. The super charged sanitary system takes solid waste and forces it down reinforced pipes at 10 gravity where it atomizes through special reversing filters transforming it into a fragrance which is soon to be a very popular unisex cologne called 'Not my Schtink; It's You.' This unique cologne will have a considerable consumer following and the sale proceeds will pay for the building's taxes. Woody even created a micro-ultrasonic air circulation system that collects dust, bacteria and viruses so each apartment room can remain almost sterile. Let the Starchitect decorate the lobby.

Now Woody has all the required signed and sealed documentation he needs and heads downtown to the building department. As he arrives on the designated floor, the waiting line seems endless and the corridor is packed to the walls. Woody then encounters a 'Take a Number' ticketing device. After getting his ticket, he walks to the back of the line and at midpoint inquires:

"How long have you been waiting?"

"Since 7 am."

Hours later, he's finally at the head of the line and enters the main room, **PERMIT REVIEW & PROCESSING**. All seats are taken; standing room only. The cacophony of different dialects is almost deafening with permit seekers scurrying around holding messy disorganized overstuffed piles of files and drawings. Every once in a while, he hears over the blasting loud speaker, a sequential number called. He looks down at his number. It's going to be a long, long wait. Each time someone exits a seat, there's a raucous race for the chair. After three hours of standing, Woody finally gets a place to sit and looks up at the clock; its 10 minutes till 4 and the department closes at 4:00 p.m. sharp. He's been there almost all day. Then he sees

Chase Mee. Remembering his last encounter, Woody tries to make amends.

"Chase, nice to see you. How are you?"

Chase is still put off by their last encounter:

"Kisser, you no my cup o' tee speakin' me the way you did. I got 10 full building permits in 30 minutes. What examiner you see?"

Woody: "I haven't been assigned to one as yet."

Chase: "Ha, ha, ha ha. I bet you here all day. Old Chinese proverb: 'Man who waits for examiner, end up with . . .'

Woody; "Cut the crap with your proverbs. I'll be back here tomorrow. Matter of fact, I might even sleep here tonight," which he does, stopping off at a vending machine, grabbing a few candy bars for diner and then curling up in a corner, using the roll of drawings as a headrest.

Its 6:00 a.m. the following day and there's already a long line waiting. The doors of the department office open 'around 8:00 am' with Woody first on line, but the crowd stampedes forward anyway. At the Receiving Desk, the clerk asks:

"You have appointment?"

Woody responds: "No."

Clerk: "You arcotek?"

Woody: "Yes I am."

"Well den, take DIS form and filla out. Whatcha here for?"

Woody responds:

"To get a new building permit."

Clerk: "Well den, take DIS form and filla out. You done environmental?"

Woody: "No."

Clerk: "Well den, take DIS form and filla out. How many stories is da building?"

Woody: "Six hundred."

Looking over the top of her glasses, the clerk says:

"I aint got no time for wise guys. I'll ax yous again: How many stories is building?"

Woody: "I'm serious. The new building will be six hundred stories."

Clerk: "Well den, take DIS form and filla out. Hey arcotek; you should also take DIS specia form and filla out. It'a for satellite interference."

Woody's thinking 'I got so many damn forms to fill out' but he fills them out and then three weeks later he has his first appointment with Gorken Gotcha. Gotcha is an old timer and has a reputation as being the toughest plan reviewer in the department. He's been with the building department for over twenty five years and has seen it all . . . until . . .

His desk not only has the all the building codes, mandates, pertinent laws, updates, revisions, et cetera, along with architectural and engineering measuring scales, rulers, magnifying glasses, but he also keeps a set of micrometers, binoculars, telescope, microscope and just in case, a urine specimen cup.

Gotcha wears old fashioned eye shades and sleeve garters. Gotcha only looks down and never makes eye contact. The meeting between Woody and Gotcha goes like this:

Gotcha: "I see you've filled out all the forms however, under type of permit requested, I've noticed the check mark you placed is not centered in the box for a new building application. Additionally, your state issued architect's rubber stamp seal is not perfectly centered in the designated box."

Woody: " Wha?"

Gotcha: "Your handwriting goes below the requisite lines."

Woody: "Wha?"

Gotcha: "And I find the ink density of your signature uneven."

Woody: "Wha ?" He thinks: 'What's this guy's problem?' What are you talking about ? I'm here for a plan review."

Gotcha: "We will begin that review after I take a mandated 15 minute yogurt break."

Exactly 15 minutes later, Gotcha returns from his break, Woody's been sitting across Gotcha's desk -- 'patiently' -- and the painful review of sheet by sheet starts.

Ever had a tooth extracted without anesthesia?

Gotcha reviews the cover sheet which consists of the project name, address and list of consultants all of which are foreign to him. He turns the cover sheet and reviews the zoning diagrams, applicable building department notes and relevant sections with references and now understands the magnitude of Woody's submission. An 8,000 foot tall, 600 story residential condominium. For the first time in his career, he picks his head up, looks up over his half glasses, adjusts his eye shade and stares into Woody's eyes. Gotcha is speechless.

"Mr. Kisser, are you the architect or expeditor for this project?"

Woody: "Architect."

Gotcha: "I'm without another word . . . er, ah" and then tries to regain his composure as an examiner, breathing deeply, adjusting his visor and reaching for a pencil, paper and calculator. Gotcha checks, re-checks and checks again all calculations. Everything is correct. But Gotcha's reputation's at stake. No one has ever gone through a plan exam with Gotcha without having numerous objections. Gotcha reaches into his metal closet and picks up a pair of binoculars and goes over to the window in his office. With his back to Woody, he says:

"I do not see any reference or calculations for the impact your building's plume will have on the troposphere or the micro climates the edifice will create. I don't see any calculations for the curvature of the earth. Your building will cast a significant shadow on coffee plantations in Columbia and Peru."

Woody: "What sections are you referencing in the building code?"

Gotcha: ***"Do you understand that I am embodiment of the building code !!? And even if it's not so stated or written, it's my opinion and decision that counts. My job is to interpret, review and comment on all aspects of building filings as they relate to the application and make adjustments and decisions where or***

when necessary. You are not to question my interpretations! Consider me the enforcer of accuracy, compliance and the Holy See of life safety, the end-all-and-be-all. Is that clear?"

Woody's on the short end of the fulcrum and not going 'to battle' with Gotcha so he sits there, uncomfortably, listening to Gotcha's incessant tirade. Gotcha takes out a dictionary and starts looking at every word for spelling mistakes while he checks: structural attachments to the earth's core; fire rating assemblies; accessibility access and turning radii; floor to floor rise, run and landings of exit stairs; measurements of the length and diameters of the handrails; coefficients of friction of floor tile; emergency lighting foot candles; energy compliance; wall sections; floor plans and distances to exits; depth of rooms to windows; window assemblies with pressure calculations; door opening resistences; corridor ventilation; bottles of beer in the refrigerator; threshold slopes, structural calculations, sections and rebar dimensions; water consumption calculations; heights of toilets, sinks and tubs; diameter of shower curtain rods, dimension of sink fittings -- Whew! -- and there's much, much more as Gotcha's acting like a detective at a crime scene looking for clues with his oversized magnifying glass.

Woody sits there patiently watching Gotcha with his various tools, red, blue, green and yellow pencils, protractors, various scales, calipers, micrometers and electron microscope, as his focused efforts continue to search for issues he can object to. Woody's looking around Gotcha's cluttered room and notices an hour glass on a wall shelf. Curiously, the hour glass has the same amount of sand in the top as in the bottom. It's not measuring time. Woody thinks back to his doctor's analogy life being like an hour glass with sand passing through it, each grain having its own sense of self-determination as Gotcha's continues his review, sheet after sheet. Woody's been sitting across Gotcha's desk since 8:00 am that morning. Apart from the yogurt break, Gotcha's scrutiny continues up until 12:00 noon when he announces he's going to take his one hour mandatory lunch break.

Gotcha's up to Sheet # 12 in a set of 300 sheets, an average of 20 minutes a sheet. It's going to be a very, very long review, particularly when Gotcha continues to use his micrometer to measure the four corners of each sheet thickness. Finally, on Sheet # 13 he sees a small diameter red splotch.

"Ha! What is this?"

Woody looks over. Gotcha perceives it as a spot of blood that he hadn't noticed before. Gotcha quickly turns the sheet page to Sheet # 14 where's there's a larger spot of red. Gotcha thumb turns a few sheets further in the set. On Sheet #28, there are a few drops of red. Woody's embarrassed.

"Well Mr. Kisser, pray tell, what am I looking at on these official documents? Bloody Lake Michigan?"

Woody's studdering kicks in.

"Er, ah, humada, ah humada, ah humada, I sincerely apologize Mr. Gotcha. I believe those tiny spots of red which you might think are drops of blood are in fact ink spots that leaked out of a pen I was using to double check, back check and re-check my work in anticipation of your reviewing my submission. Your reputation precedes you."

Woody's trying to give some 'face' and respect to Gotcha.

Gotcha, maintaining his demeanor says:

"Well, in all my years as the chief plan examiner, no one has ever had a review without numerous objections. So back to business. I will temporarily overlook the ink spots as you say they are and come back to them after I finish." Gotcha, however, pulls out an ultraviolet light to check for blood fluorescence, just in case and adjusts his eye shade and half glasses as he continues his meticulous scrutiny.

As 4:00 p.m. approaches, Gotcha prepares himself to conclude the day. Scanning over his half glasses, he says:

"Mr. Kisser, we will pick this up again tomorrow morning at 8:00 a. m. sharp. Here is a pass that you are to show Rotunda when you enter Permit Processing and Review. That is all for now."

Woody starts to ask a question but Gotcha abruptly cut's him off.

"It's 4:01p.m., Mr. Kisser. I am finished for the day."

Woody thinks: 'What a fricken douche bag this asshole is. I'll be here forever.' He heads for the exit. At the elevator bank he bumps into Chase Mee.

"Kisser. I see you draw unlucky straw, he,he ."

"What are you taking about?" Woody asks.

"Gotcha you plan reviewer."

Chase, through his contacts at the department, made behind-the-scenes arrangements for Gotcha to review Woody's submission.

"Had you pay me 50 gees, no problem with dick head. Old Chinese proverb 'Man who go to bed with problem in hand, wake up with solution in palm.' Ha Ha Ha! Woody just doesn't respond and leaves. He's resolute about sitting through the exam and getting his building permit. Woody returns to his 'home office' -- (where else is he going to go?)

On his way there, he passes a newsstand where bold tabloids headline:

DEVELOPER CAUGHT
DOMICILE DAMAGED BY
DERANGED DRAGONESS

There's a photo of Sy Philis's wife Sylvia, horrified, with a rolling pin so tightly held that the veins are popping in her hand while she talks to police officers. The police are pleading with her to drop it, but she can't.

A sub caption to the scoop reads:

Slum Lord Caught With Secretary

Woody picks up the paper.

Article: Sylvia Philis, wife of noted slum lord Sy Philis finds her husband in bed with Moaner Fordic. Moaner Fordic, part time actress, part time cocktail waitress, part time cruise ship entertainer, part time pole dance, part time meter maid, part time pencil sharpener and part time secretary to developer Sy Philis, were found in bed together in the apartment shared by the Philises. In an interview with a reporter, Sy Philiis has completely denied any wrongdoing and alleged that his poor, unfortunate, medicated wife is suffering psychological aberrations. "No such thing would ever happen," he claimed. Sy's to remember a well-referenced quote and screws it up.

"I've been married to the same woman for 40 years. Why would I go out for a nice piece of fresh pie when I can have the same old stuffed fruit cake I can get at home?"

Woody's reading more of the salacious details that typically appeal to the tabloid's readers:

Sy's popped extra E.D. tablets to keep pace with Moaner who's just going through the gyrations, on cruise control and faking passionate exhilaration as she grabs Sy's hair and accidently pulls off his wig; Sy's heart's pounding away as his body contorts. Bed sheets asunder, Sy's experiencing pre-mature rigor mortis. Of course, those details were really not in the news, but you probably wanted to know what was happening.

Woody takes the paper and trashes it, hoping someone uses it to pick up dog doody. He's not surprised that Moaner has hooked up with Philis. They deserve each other. Once back at his office, which has the appearance of having been struck by a tornado, Woody attempts to straighten out the mess of papers strewn about and contemplates the next day with Gotcha as he settles into a sleeping bag for an uncomfortable night on the floor. He sets his alarm watch for 5:30 am so he can be at the building department early enough and prepared for whatever Gotcha might throw at him. It's hard for Woody to unwind as he tries both physical and mental distractions - including pulling his pud- to relax his body. Neither technique works. He is now wondering what will come first; his death from brain cancer or his inability to get Philis's building permit on the contracted 'date certain.'

He wonders about the static state of the hour glass in Gotcha's office and if there's some meaning as to why there are equal amounts of sand in the top and bottom portions but he'll hold his question until such time as it's opportune to ask.

It's early morning the next day and Woody heads off to the building department. He stops at a small coffee shop picking up a quart of the strongest octane caffeine. He slips into an alleyway, pulls out a syringe and mainlines the solution so he can keep his edge in preparation of Gotcha's vigilance.

Across the street from the alley is a small dusty shop that sells old, used and outdated items including medical and dental instruments and other nonessential things. In the window is a special sphinctometer, hooked together with a personality trait examiner and bull shit detector. It's only 3 bucks and the wiring's old, but Woody wants it. Also on display is a nerdometer but he doesn't think he has much use for it. So the 160 octane caffeine kicks as Woody enters the building department's Permit Review and Processing room.

He shows the pass Gotcha gave him to Rotunda who rotates her eyeballs towards the ceiling in an expression of consternation and Woody proceeds towards Gotcha's office. It's 7:30 in the morning as Woody, standing in the threshold, observes Gotcha wearing a blindfold, orchestrating his way around his office as Wagners' Meistersinger' music blasts. Woody dare not enter until beckoned at 8 a.m. so he waits and watches the show.

Woody thinks Gotcha's certifiable. Precisely at 8:00, Gotcha's at his desk, arm garters and eye shade in place. He permits Woody's entrance and motions him to sit down and on Day 2, the review process continues, as Gotcha starts with Sheet #15. Woody is sitting there fidgeting, trying to manage his hyper-caffeinated state. All of a sudden, the 'top twenty stories' within Woody's body comes 'crashing down to his body's cellar'; he has a pressing need for a relieving facility so asks:

"Mr. Gotcha, is there a restroom nearby? And I mean. very nearby?"

No response, as if Gotcha doesn't hear him.

"MR.GOTCHA – SIR – IS THERE A DAMN RESTROOM NEARBY?"

Gotcha raises his head slightly as he looks over his half glasses.

"Take the stairs up two flights; make a left at the exit, down the hall on the right make another right and then a left where you'll see the public restrooms. The access code is: TangoAlphaKiloEchoAlphaSierraHotelIndiaTango1234321. Got it?"

Woody's never heard of anything like this, can't remember what Gotcha said and makes a mad dash out of Permit Review & Processing as he bolts down the stairs. Halfway down, he realizes he was supposed to take two stair flights up. Out of breath, with his eyeballs floating, he asks everyone in the hallway:

"Restroom? Restroom? please!"

He's running around a labyrinth. Finally, at the locked door to the men's room, and not remembering the access code, pulling the door handle out of frustration, his fortune turns. Someone is exiting at that lucky moment and Woody gets entry and is ultimately relieved. Twenty minutes later, he's back at Gotcha's desk. Gotcha has advanced to Sheet #17.

Gotcha: "The kerning between the lettering on the wall section D6/17 is inconsistent. Is there a reason for that?"

Woody leans over the sheet to get a better look as he searches for a fast answer to such a ridiculous question.

"Mr. Gotcha, the variation in the letter spacing exists because as represented in that section, the air space between the brick and substrate will vary in micrometer widths as a result of the back side of the brick not being truly flat and I thought that fact should be reflected in the space between the letters."

'What a crock of shit.'

Gotcha likes what he hears:

"Mr. Kisser, you might be the first architect with whom I've reviewed a submission with who cares about the translation of design intent as it is represented graphically combined with the integration of the written description.

'Another crock.'

Woody senses an opening of camaraderie with Gotcha but it turn out to be short-lived as Gotcha goes back to Sheet #3 where symbols, notes, labels, descriptions and references are listed. Gotcha flips back and forth between Sheet #3 and Sheet #17 and focuses on the graphic symbol for brick on Sheet #3 and the brick wall section on Sheet #17.

"Mr. Kisser, I noticed another major discrepancy. The symbols for brick differ. Are you trying to 'pull a fast one' on me?"

Woody: "May I look?"

Woody sees no apparent difference, whereby Gotcha lifts the electron microscope off the floor. In a commanding voice, Gotcha says:

"Mr. Kisser; please look very carefully through my electron microscope at the textural representation of brick shown on Sheet #3 and on Sheet #17. See how they differ? Can you explain?"

Woody's thinking: 'What's this guy's fuckin' problem?' but he stays on track, answering:

"Sir, as you well know, brick is a manufactured product of our planet, clay specifically, and as a result, has inconsistent molecular configurations caused by the release of free electrons in the water content ratio and again, I felt it necessary to create a graphic deviation to bring this to light.

Gotcha places his hand to cradle his chin and thinks about Woody's answer.

"Okay. I'll accept that" and then he turns to Sheet #18.

Woody thinks: 'At the pace of this review, the ice caps will melt, flood the earth and eliminate all existence. Maybe I should build an ark.'

And Gotcha, first using his micrometer to measure sheet thickness. continues his laborious review. Woody hasn't had anything to eat but multiple candy bars from the vending machine. His blood sugar level blows past medical abnormalities as his whole body shows signs of nutritional negligence that are growing more dire by the minute. He's starting to resemble a werewolf as his irises whiten.

He asks Gotcha for the access code to the restroom again, taking an indelible marker and writing it out on his forearm for the next time he needs it. And he sits there, agonizing, waiting, waiting and waiting as Gotcha fuddles with measuring devices, dividers, a 20x magnifying glass and a dictionary.

It's now Day 6 at Permit Review & Processing, where Woody's sitting across from Gotcha who is now on Sheet #70. Woody's wearing mirrored sunglasses so he can catch a few winks as he sits there. He even made a contraption brace out of coat hangers hidden within his jacket to keep from falling over if he nods out. Woody's tries experimenting with relaxing his eyes, alternating shutting one eye while keeping the other open, but it doesn't work for long as he starts to drift away.

All of a sudden, his cell phone rings which startles him and Gotcha.

Gotcha: "Mr. Kisser: do you see that sign behind me?"

Woody looks. It's a small sign that was blocked by Gotcha's body. It reads:

NO

CELL PHONES - ELECTRONIC DEVICES –

PROFANITY - SMOKING – CHEWING GUM

WATER BOTTLES – HAIR COMBING – TOOTHPICKING –

VOLLEYBALL - EYEBALL MAINTENANCE IS FORBIDDEN!!!!!

100% FOCUS AND ATTENTION IS MANDATORY

***

To the unknowing, eyeball maintenance is the activity where one closes their eyes to carefully look for very tiny holes in their eyelids, (a/k/a sleeping). Woody apologizes.

"Mr. Gotcha, this might be an important call regarding this project. May I be excused, Sir, and I sincerely apologize for both the interruption and not noticing the sign behind your desk."

Gotcha lifts his head from the sheet he's reviewing and with significant scorn, says:

"Let this be first and last time; understood? Now take your call outside my office and never again – I repeat never again - allow my focus to be interrupted. Are we clear?"

Woody: "Yes, sir."

He goes outside to take the call.

The caller's number is listed as Restricted.

It turns out to be Sy Philis.

"Kisser, what's the status of my building permit? I heard a new code is about to be enacted that'll become enforceable if you don't have full building department approvals by next Monday. That's in 5 days. What's the status?"

Woody: "I'm at the building department right now. We're reviewing Sheet #70 of 300. I've been here for the past two weeks sitting in front of an examiner."

"You're what...? Expediting my project yourself? Are you a damn fool? Why didn't you use someone who knows the 'ropes' down there? You'll miss the deadline and I'm going to hold you accountable!"

Woody responds:

"Philis; you know how much money you owe me and promised I'd get paid? Plus you expect me to hire a permit expeditor and pay them with what? Blood? I've been breaking my ass, living in my office, working day and night to finish the drawings and you have the nerve to talk to me this way?"

And now the discussion heats up further.

"Let me tell you something Kisser; I will have your ass. And I will have your license taken away for incompetence. I'll have you run out of townn. You won't be allowed to clean a dog pound cage. You don't know who you're talking to, you ungrateful piece of shit. You keep distracting our conversation back to money. Your check is in the mail! I don't run the postal service. I'm so

damn fed up with your crybaby antics. I might have to take matters into my own hands."

With that, Sy hangs up.

Woody goes back inside to sit with Gotcha and expects another scolding.

Gotcha: "Mr. Kisser, I must say, I find your drawing extremely thorough and complete, but only to this point. What I find later in my review might, however, change my mind."

"Mr. Gotcha, may I ask you a question?"

Gotcha: "Yes."

"Sir, I heard something that I consider might be just a rumor which I wanted to pass by you."

Gotcha: "What is it?"

Woody: "I preface my question, again with 'I heard a rumor.' Is there going to be a change in the building code that will come into effect next Monday - five days from today - that regardless of where a submission is in the review process, if one does not have a building permit in hand, the new code will become enforceable. Sir – Is that correct?"

Gotcha: "Yes – why do you ask?"

Woody: "Well – sir – at the rate of this review – it's likely to go past next Monday."

Gotcha: "Had you submitted your documents six months ago, you might have a permit now."

Woody's thinking: 'I didn't even start this ridiculous project until six weeks ago.' He asks:

"Mr. Gotcha, is there any way I can hope to have my review completed before next Monday?"

Gotcha: "No, no and no. Mr. Kisser, I have a reputation to uphold. No one gets through a plan review without objections. Do you understand that? Although I'm only on Sheet #70, and there are many more sheets to scrutinize, I can predict with absolute certainty, I will find objections."

Just then, a phone rings from inside Gotcha's desk. He opens a drawer, pulls out a red phone and picks up the receiver as he cups his hand over speaking end. "Mr. Kisser, please excuse me. I must take this call. Please leave my office immediately and wait in the ante room."

Woody's surprised, gets up and leaves Gotcha's office. In the ante room he can hear Gotcha:

"Yes sir, yes sir. No sir, no sir. No. Yes sir. No. Understood. Completely sir. Good day to you."

A few moment pass and Gotcha summons Woody back into his office and motions him to sit down. Gotcha takes out his inhaler and with his cheeks full, exhales and looks downwards.

"Mr. Kisser, it is my opinion, based on the consistent quality, accuracy and attention to detail of the 70 sheets of drawings I've reviewed to date, that the rest of the 230 sheets in your submission are in compliance with the current building code and I therefore ceremoniously anoint my signature to my official stamp of approval. Go forth and build your edifice."

Woody sits there stunned. Who is this guy, who for weeks, was putting me through the wringer and suddenly gives me full approval on drawings he didn't even look at? What is going on? This is very strange. Woody's wondering if the phone call Gotcha received had anything to do with his sudden reversal. Woody goes through thePermit Review & Processing to get his drawings finalized whereby Rotunda, the clerk, asks for a check. It's in the thousands of dollars. Woody obviously doesn't have any money so he calls Sy.

Sy then asks for the name of the clerk, gets it and hangs up. One minute later, Rotunda's cell phone rings and says to Woody:

"Excuse me, I have to take this."

And Woody hears Rotunda responding: "Yes it is. Fine and you? Of course. Yes. Silver Blue convertible with chrome wheels. Automatic, not stick. Okay. Yes. The same to you. Bye."

Rotunda: "Mitta Arcotek ; your permit's been taken care of. Have a nice day."

Woody's again confused. A few minutes ago, the clerk was asking him to pay for his new building permit and now it's taken care of? What's going on? Woody leaves the building department and as he walks back to his office, he sees the bold tabloid headlines plastered over the news stand:

SOS

Sylvia Ousts Sy

Sues for Divorce – Major Project at Risk – Sy sends out Distress Signals

SyPhilis, well-known slumlord was found cavorting in bed with his secretary by his wife Sylvia Philis. Ms. Phyilis, a seasoned, experienced attorney, well known for her large hats, loud voice and shar- biting tenacity has gained a fierce reputation over the years in women's rights specializing in divorce, never compromising an iota and winning billions of dollars in divorce settlements. Sylvia Philis is feared more than famine, death and bad breath. Sylvia wants Sy's properties, including his plans to erect the tallest residential building ever constructed. Sy named his building: 'The Saturnscraper.' Sylvia plans to change the name of the building to The Schuntzy – named after her miniature dog she carries around in her purse along with a burdizzo, which is a handheld held device that castrates bulls.

The following week Woody gets a call from Sylvia Philis. She asks the design team of Les and Woody to attend a meeting in her office. Woody arrives at Sylvia's office first at the scheduled time and is escorted in to her conference room, which is decorated in a unique style called 'rococo gone mad.' He sits there trying to take in the over-the-top, over-stuffed and overdone décor. 30 minutes later, Les, wearing an outrageous floral cape and a cavalier hat with peacock embellishments enters carrying a single rose:

"Voody- how nissce to see you. This place is gorgeous! Sylvia follows carrying her miniature dog. Les gives her the single rose and slathers her with compliments.

"Sylvia – this place is absoooolutely ssscccrumptiss. Oh my God! I feel as if I'm in heaven. What's the name of precious little cutsie? I love his diamond studded mink coat and painted toenails."

Sylvia responds to Les. "So you're the Starchitect I've heard so much about. You should be very proud.. And thank you for the beautiful rose. It'll be perfect at home in my Louis XIVcrystal vase. My baby's name is Schuntzy; I had him neutered."

Woody thinks: 'Poor mutt. Wearing a diamond-studded mink coat, painted toenails and no balls. Sylvia then turns to Woody:

"And I assume you're the mechanic – er, I mean – the architect of record," extending her thickly covered jeweled hand.

"Yes ma'am – I am."

"Please sit down; would you like an afternoon tea?"

Les: "Oh what a delightful idea. I'll have jasmine with a whisper of mint."

Woody's thinking 'Tea can't even prime my pump.' He says:

"No thank you."

Sylvia continues in her loud voice: "So, I've asked both of you here to tell you that I'm taking over Sy's project. Would you each explain your roles since I've never done anything like this before?"

Les jumps in before Sylvia can finish her sentence.

"Sylvia, I'm the designer, conceptualist, visionary and creator of what will be the most sssought after residential condo project in town. You'll be the feature in every upper class magazine. Your building will be completely bathed in total elegance, inside and out. The exterior pink talc panels will be such a wonderful counterpoint to the drab brick and granite you see . . ."

Sylvia cuts him off and turns to Woody:

"And *you?* What's your role?"

"Ms. Philis, I am the architect of record."

Sylvia: "Now I'm confused. Why do I need two architects on the same project?"

Moments of silence. Les is starting to feel uncomfortable.

"Sylvia, that's the way your husband set it up."

Sylvia to Les: "Les, since you created the concept, I think you should be the architect of record and I see no need for the other."

Turning to Woody, Sylvia says: "I didn't get your name, however, I see no need for your services. Thank you. You may leave now."

Woody: "Ms. Philis, I've already filed the set and received a building permit."

Sylvia then turns to Les:

"Why didn't you do it?"

Les has never filed a set of construction drawings and now feels put on the spot. Sylvia's starting to get agitated. Les says:

"Sylvia, I develop cutting-edge, fashionable building concepts and the more mundane aspects such as constru . . ."

Sylvia summarily cuts him off.

"Refer to me as 'Ms. Philis. We are not on a first name basis. I want to know why you are not the architect of record."

Les' voice shrinks to a tiny sound as he tries to maintain some stature/

"Ms. Philis, I've never taken on that role. Clients hire me for my extraordinary brilliance, not my understanding of the way things work. I'm more of an artist of buildings."

Sylvia: "I want to know who I sue when I have problems. You or the other guy – sorry I forgot your name again. Explain to me, what is your role as the architect of record?"

Woody: "Well ma'am, simply stated, I take someone's idea of a building and translate that into construction documents that can be both permitted and used to build from. I make sure the design is in compliance with zoning. that the design including the plans, materials and all other criteria meet the building code and are properly constructible and I coordinate and guide all the engineering consultants – structural, mechanical, plumbing, electrical, landscape and others - to eliminate conflicts and to make sure all the scopes of their work are covered, conform to the current building code. And then I file for permits, make site visits during construction, review and comment on shop drawings, respond to contractors questions, review and approve their requisitions for payment and walk through to make sure the contractor built what I drew and you contracted for. There's much more that I do as the architect of record, but for brevity's' sake . . ."

Sylvia: "It seems to me that my decorator can do what the 'Floral Capeman' over their does." She points at Les. Woody pauses.

"Your name is, again, please?"

"Woody Kisser," he responds.

"Mr. Kisser, please explain to me why you're not considered a Starchitect, given that you seem to know everything. What am I missing?"

"Frankly, I don't have a public relations firm with world-class media connections representing my work, and I don't get invited to the right parties. It's not that I can't create imaginative and provocative buildings."

"So you're going to spend the rest of your professional life making others look good?"

Reaching into her purse, Sylvia pulls out the burdizzo.

Woody looks: "What is *that*?"

Sylvia: "It's a tool to render you 'inept,' which you'll be if you continue down this road."

She turns to Les, who is shriveled up in the corner, sucking on his thumb.

"Ismore, I think it's time for you to leave, cape and all."

Now Les is having a major meltdown.

"I want my mommy!" holding his cape like a blanky.

Woody: "Ms. Philis, please note that I haven't been paid a dime to date for my services."

Sylvia: "Sounds typical of Sy. I'll take that up with you another time. I've had enough of this circus. See my secretary and arrange for another appointment.

Woody leaves and on his way back to his home office sees a homemade paper advertisement, with tear off number tabs along the bottom, taped to the leg of the statue of Zeus.

For The Most Creative Web Design Ever: 'You Dream It – I'll Scheme It'

Woody takes the phone number and calls it. He hears:C

"CockadoodledoWakeUp Bro' -- you know what to do. Beep."

Woody's never heard a phone answered like that, but leaves his name and number for a call back. Was this a mistake? The next day Woody's cell phone rings and he answers it. The name of the caller is Wazupp. Wazupp's got a web design service called: cockadoodledoWakeUp Bro'.com. For a reasonable fee, Wazupp will design a very imaginative, provocative and cutting-edge website if you meet his requirements. Woody checks out Wazupp's sample websites. The various websites are unusual, dramatically different from what he's ever seen before. Woody becomes fascinated by Wazupp's manipulation of the medium. So they meet, in a diner, of course.

Wazupp shows up and has a fro' the size of a hot air balloon; wears one white sneaker, the other's black, a mouth grille that spells out WAZUPP on each tooth and Woody feels a need to settle in on Wazupp's appearance, but he quickly gets past it. The conversation goes something like this:

Wazupp starts with a rap:

"Yo bro, I see you checking out my fro, makes me think you got no dough, ax my mammy, she said don't go, but I says so and dat's all I know."

Woody's confused. Is this guy legit? Could he really have created such extraordinary web sites?

Woody: "Mr. Wazupp, I called you after I saw some of the incredible websites you designed. Did you create them? Please be honest; I don't have much time."

All of a sudden, Wazupp removes his 'fro' which reveals a short slicked back 'doo." His tooth grille is gone. He puts on very thick nerd glasses whereby he transforms into a computer geek.

Woody's taken aback. "What is this about, Mr. Wazzup?"

Wazzup says: "My real name is God."

Woody responds: "What? Are you fucking crazy? You think you're God?"

God: "No. I said that my name is God but I am not God as you probably think of God. It's a unique name nobody else uses. Iit separates me from everyone else. Remember, it's just a name. You can call me Joe, Xerces or Rayne Maiker if that'll make you feel more comfortable. I can create any website you wish."

Woody: "So what's with the clown costume?"

God: "I use it to see if someone has predispositions towards stereotypes. I only take on certain types of clients."

Woody: "What's that about?"

God: "I only like to work with people who have positive karma. If you have biases; I feel negative ions."

Woody's think 'this guy's a fricken nut job' but he decides to go along with it anyway.

"You mean you can create a website so people will consider me a Starchitect? You can do it?"

God: "Of course I can. I can create anything on the web. But I'm not familiar with the term Starchitect. Please explain."

Woody: "Well, it's a new term that, er, I, um, it's a term used by the media and developers to promote their residential buildings. Most condo buyers feel that if a starchitect designed their residence, the residence has to be very special. Developers use a starchitect as a lure."

God:" So what do you do?"

Woody: "I take someone else's concept of a building and then create all the working documents, details, specifications and so on so that it can be built. I also file for the appropriate permits."

God: "Who hires you?"

Woody: "Typically, the developer of the project."

God: "And what does this developer refer to you as?"

Woody: "The Architect of Record."

God: "So as I understand it, you do all the work and have all the responsibility – but get little credit. Is that correct?"

Woody: "In a nutshell – yes."

God: "Whew!" So you're asking me to develop a website that makes you a starchitect – yes?"

Woody: "Yes."

God: "This is an easy lift since this is not a transformative event."

God and Woody agree on a fee and both leave the diner and head in opposite directions. Woody's thinking 'I now know what a towel must feel like during the spin cycle of a washing machine.'

Just then, Woody's cell phone rings. It's Sylvia Philis, speaking very formally:

"Woodward, come to my office now please. I want you to meet someone." And Woody starts heading over to Sylvia's. Arriving at Sylvia's office he's again greeted and escorted into the rococo-gone-mad conference room. Moments later, Sylvia walks in embracing her very small dog in one arm and in her other arm, guess who? Busta Urchin.

Busta Urchin has gone through a total makeover including a change of name. Busta's well shaven, crewcut, dressed in a nice suit and tie, fake architect's glasses and polished brogues. Gone are the multiple neck bracelets, finger rings and tattoos.

Sylvia: "Woodard, I'd like you to meet Al Dente. He owns Acne Construction and has an impressive portfolio of residential projects. Mr. Dente approached me after he heard I took control of Sy's project and I found him to be quite knowledgeable. Not that I know anything about construction, but I'd like the both of you to sit and discuss how to go forward.

Sylvia leaves the room.

Woody shuts the door and says: "Busta. What the fuck are you doing here, you fucking lowlife? I kicked you out of my office and you show up *here?* And what's with the outfit, glasses and name change? Who do you think you're kidding?"

Busta: "Look Woody, I've got to make a living and the only field I know is buildin' construction. Can't we keep this between ourselves? Please don't tro me under da bus."

Woody: "Are you still serving knuckle sandwiches to those you don't get along with?"

Busta: "Buildin' construction is a tough business and sometimes 'ya gotta do what ya gotta do."

Woody: "Well, you better leave me far away from your knuckle busting shenanigans. So why are you here?"

Busta:" Woody, yous gotta start calling me Al, so as not to confuse Sylvia. I need da' job."

Woody: "Okay Al, so why are you here?"

"I told Sylvia I can bring lotsa value, buying da' job out, watching her piggybank, value engineerin'et. cetera. You do have the buildin' permit – right?"

Woody: "I was wondering about that. I ended up with the worst plan examiner who scrutinized everything down to the line widths and sheet thicknesses and all of a sudden, after spending every day of many weeks sitting through agonizing psychological pain, he gets a phone call. The phone by the way is a special phone, stored in his desk drawer and its red, like the one POTUS has and Gotcha answers it. All I hear is 'Yyes; yes; yes, and then moments later after he hangs up, he approves my application, without even looking at the rest of the 230 sheets in the set."

Al: "You were being examined by Gotcha."

Woody: "Yup."

Al: "All I can tell you is that Gotcha's got some issues only a few know about."

Woody: "Oh! Is there some . . ."

Al summarily cuts him off.

"Don't ask!"

Woody: "What happened with STD?"

Al: "I still have it – not going away."

Woody: "So what's with Acne Construction?"

Al: "I also werk 'dare as a project manager and on-site rep to fill in the gaps."

Woody: "So are you on 'board'?"

Al: "I tink so. Mrs. Philis wasn't too happy finding 'ol Sy playin' 'hide the sayseech' with Moaner Fordic. I called her when she got control of the buildin'."

A few minutes pass and then Sylvia walks in:

"Okay boys, where do we go from here?"

Al: "Me and Woody are in total sync how to go forwad' and wez ready to go when you 'push the start button'."

Sylvia; "Will the building have purified water for my Schnutzy?"

Al: "Mrs. Philis, your buildin' will have everythin' you can imagine and more."

Sylvia: "Great. Where's the start button Al?"

Al: "Jus shake my hand and sign these contracts."

Sylvia: "I think I should review them first."

Sylvia takes them and walks out. Woody and Al look at each other with puzzlement, both leave as well. A few days later, Woody gets a call from God who asks him to come over to his studio to review a draft of God's website design. Woody shows up at God's studio, where he is offered an espresso and a nice comfortable chair to sit back and watch God's creation on a large format screen.

<u>Opening slide</u>:
The World's Greatest Architect
<u>Second slide</u>:
Deeh Itie

Third slide:
The Most Strikingly Magnificent Unusual Buildings Never Before Seen
Fourth slide:
People Who Live In His Building Do Not Age
Fifth slide:
Lose Weight - Regrow Hair If Lost
Sixth slide:
Become Worry Free - Are Always Happy - Never Argue
Seventh slide:
Eat - Drink - Smoke & Have High Cholesterol Diets
Eighth slide:

Mr. Itie creations are unique residential buildings that combine form, materials, karma and advanced induction technology systems that include collagen, testosterone, complex vitamins and planetary spirits along with high fiber inducted air systems by means of which the occupants experience retarded aging, lose weight and live better, healthier lives. Additionally, it's been noticed that the occupants are free from any anxiety or depression and do not take any medications. All inhabitants of Deeh Itie's building are continuously ecstatic. And the views are 'to die for' but you don't and won't.

Ninth and next ten slides:

Collage of different buildings and interiors.

Woody: "God, tell me; what's with the name 'Deeh Itie' and 'those who live in such a building don't age?"

God: "Woody, what type of splash do you want to make?"

Woody: "what do you mean - splash?"

God: "Do you want to make a splash like a tiny pebble or a single grain of sand dropped into a lake where you see one small single ripple ring or a meteorite that dropped into the ocean and creates a tsunami?"

Woody's thinking 'Again with a tiny grain of sand. What do I have to lose' "God, make a *big* splash; that's what life's about!"

God: "You now understand. The website I design for you will do just that."

Woody leaves and for the first time, in a very long time, feels exalted and heads back to his home office where he starts to clean up the mess of papers, coffee filled IV bags and various magazines of distraction. He wonders if anyone of those single grains of sand in his life's hour glass contributed to what he considers to be the luck of having found God. Woody then gets a message from God:

Woody, I've taken the liberty to give you a new identity and contact information. Go forth, be well and be careful what you wish for. Best, God.

Woody's wondering about his new identity and contact information. He goes 'on line' to check out 'theworldsgreatsstarchitect.com' and sees the website of The World's Greatest Starchitect.

The website is God's best-ever design. God has created images of buildings and interiors that are so extraordinary that all other starchitects' residential projects pale greatly in comparison. God has included a toll free number as well; calls to it are automatically forwarded to Woody's cell.

All of a sudden, the press picks up the news of this '*never before heard of starchitect*' and runs with it, big time. Headline:

HEAVEN ON EARTH

UNKNOWN ARCHITECT CREATES TIMELESS BUILDING FOR THE AGELESS

> *Deeh Itie, anarchitect unknown except to his mother, has created the most amazing residential buildings. Using the most advanced technologies, the residents of his building do not age, become free of medications, lose weight, et cetera, et cetera.*

Rabid Pharmaceutical, one of the pharmaceutical giants, gets wind of this from their public relations firm, Phulla Gasse. Rabid shows its fangs and now tries to discredit and counteract the virtues of living in a Dee Itie's designed building. Rabid Pharma's marketing department fears that a mass exodus towards Dee Itie's buildings will result in a significant drop off in prescription drug sales.

But Woody is undeterred. After cleaning up his office, he decides to treat himself to a steak dinner. As he prepares to leave, four messengers wheel in a four foot by eight foot skid of one thousand shop drawings piled as high as the door to his office. They're all marked The SCHUNTZY with a transmittal from Al Dente which Sylvia's copied on in large print: 'I NEED BACK IN THREE DAYS'.

Woody asks the messengers to hold on as he quickly goes through the heap. He breaks the submission in half which the messengers take to Les's office. Woody's thinking: 'I know Dente's game.' He sent 'out of sequence' shop drawing submittals so as to claim a delay. Why would I want to look at kitchen cabinet hardware shop drawings and paint samples when I need basic building foundation shop drawings first?

Later, Woody gets a call from Les:

"Voody, I received a huge pile of papers addressed to you that were delivered to me. Why am I getting it? What is this, pray tell? Its' certainly not wall paper? And I can't go through it now because I just had a manicure and my nail polish isn't dry!"

Woody: "Les, what I sent are shop drawings I need you to comment on."

Les: "What do you mean when you say 'these are shop drawings'? Are they from Swishers' Fine Haberdashery Shop where I ordered a new designers cape from?"

"No!!" replies Woody, "What I sent you are the submissions from different contractors that I need you to mark up and stamp either approved, not approved or resubmit."

Les: "Stamp with what - my sisshoe?"

Woody: "No! Your shop drawing stamp. Don't you have one?"

"Voodvard, I haven't the faintest idea what you are talking about."

Woody's now getting exasperated. "Les, do you have a shop drawing stamp that you use to comment on when contractors make submissions to you?"

Les: "Oh, you mean if the wall paper isn't flocked enough, how do I respond?"

Woody: "Yes! When a contractor sends you flocked wall paper you don't like, how do you respond?"

Les: "Voodard, using rubber stamps is soooooooooo old fasshioned. Just forget it! I use emoticon stickers."

Woody: "You use what...?"

"Voodvard, get with it, sissister! You don't use a quill pen and an inkwell to write, do you?"

Woody's thinking: 'What planet did this guy come from?' He then goes through the submissions he kept, marking them up accordingly. Next he gets a call from Al Dente.

"Woody, hows yas doin'? When does I gets my 'shops' back?"

Woody: "Al, you're flooding me with out of sequence shop drawings so you can claim I'm delaying the project by not returning them back to you within the three day window. Where's your submission schedule?"

Al, evading the question, says: "Yous keepin' the log –right?"

Woody knows there'll be no 'winning' with the likes of Al, so he'll play the game as well, circling sheets with a red pen, adding question marks, writing 'not clear' and stamping the shop drawings '**RESUBMIT**' and then sending them back to Al. This will be a constant merry-go round but Woody's been on this ride before. And the next day another four foot by eight foot skid of shop drawings shows up. Looking through it, shower curtain rods, toilet paper holders, soap dishes, et cetera, Woody's getting frustrated.

He calls Al: "Why are you sending me these shop drawings? Are we building a building or decorating a bathroom?"

Al: "Ms. Phylis is working with a desecrator and she told me that the effort should be put into what the residents 'see' and to focus on getting those contractors on board first."

So Woody calls Sylvia and asks for a meeting. Her secretary sets it up and the meeting in the 'rococo gone mad' conference room goes as follows:

Woody: "Ms Phylis, thank you for taking the time to meet with me."

Sylvia: "Woodward, I have exactly four minutes and twenty three seconds; what would you like?"

"Ms. Phylis, I'm receiving shop drawings from Al Dente that are out of sequence. He said you wanted him to focus on the finishes fir . . ."

Sylvia: "Woodward, I have no idea what you're talking about. What is a shop drawing?"

Woody: "A shop drawing is a submission from a contractor that describes in detail via a drawing, or a physical sample, how something will be fabricated, finished, assem . . ."

Sylvia: "Woodward, please get to the point."

Woody: "Ms. Phylis, Al Dente told me you told him to get . . ."

Sylvia interrupts: "Woodard – "I told, you told blah blah blah; work it all out with Undercooked Ziti, or whatever his name is. I have a law practice to run. I told him my decorator knows best. That's it; good day."

'Whew – she's tough!' Woody thinks as he heads back to his home office. Under his door is an envelope sealed with a wax embossment and no return address. Woody holds the envelope over a lamp to see if there are any signs of anthrax or other toxic powders. It's filled with rose petals. Woody very carefully opens the envelope with a razor blade. It's from Moaner and reads as follows:

> Dear Woody:
>
> *I'd like to apologize for my behavior and the way I spoke when I last left your office. I learned a lot while working for you. I've decided to pursue a career in real estate development with a great company and need a letter of reference. Would you kindly write one?*
>
> *All the best,*
> Moaner Fordic.

Woody's thinking: 'Moaner's going into the real estate development business? I guess you don't need any experience. Just the right contacts, and access to money along with personality which Moaner certainly has plenty of. Human nature's funny; when someone wants something from you, how quickly they change their tone.

Had I needed anything from her, I could have guessed her response.'

Woody calls Al and suggests a meeting to sort out the sequencing of shop drawings issues. They meet and Al is in a more agreeable mood.

Al: "Woody, dars a few tings I doesn't understand. Please explain me."

Woody: "Sure. What do you not understand?"

Al: "Well, for one, at da top of da buildin' ders dis steel ball filled with uranium or sumptim' wid dees big fricken springs all around. Wha dis for?"

Woody: "That's called a tuned mass dampener that'll counteract the sway of the building."

Al: "You means if I lived in the penthouse and I was looking nort, I could see Canada den da buildin' swayed back, I could see da nort pole and versa visa?"

Woody: "Yes, but the dampener is designed to significantly reduce that effect."

Al: "Whew! I knows that feelin' wen I had too many beers and end up prayin ta 'da porcelain gods'."

Woody: "What?"

Al: "And da special reversin gizmo dat prevents satellites from bangin' into the tower, who would want to live dare anyways?"

Woody: "Folks with lots and lots of money who want to see the sunrise in Europe and sunset in Asia."

Al: "I guess dem folks don't like ta sleep. Must be up 'schtupin'."

Woody: "I wouldn't know. When am I going to get the foundation submission?"

Al: "I wanted to ax you about dat. I spoke to my guy about drillin' thru da... whatama'callit ....mantle of da erth. He saw one of dem science shows where the erth's hot and he's worried 'bout meltin' his drill bits."

Woody: "Have your driller go to hardshaft.com where he can find Extra Hardened Shafts that can take the heat."

Al: "Dats good to know. Whas da' name again?"

A few weeks later, there's significant activity on the site with surveyors, astrophysics, astrologists, geologists, acupuncturists, star gazers, experts, decedents of Newton, Archimedes, Copernicus and Galileo etc. mingling around the quilted metal food cart. One of Newton's descendants, Phyg, orders an apple and drops it. Gabby Blabla, Sylvia's decorator shows up in a dress and very high heels. She stays on the sidelines. Al takes command:

"Listen up! Everyone; sign in and ya puts ya hardhats on yis lids!"

He looks at Gabby, who yells out:

"Are you Al Dente?"

Al: "Depends what yis lookin' fer."

Gabby: "I'm here representing Sylvia Philis. Is there a ladies room I can use to freshen up?"

Al: "Wez got field terlits yous can use over dare, but you ain't allowed on da site wid dem high heel shoes."

Gabby: "I've never heard of such a thing. I've decorated over one hundred apartments and never been told that."

Moments later, Al's cell phone rings; it's Sylvia:

"Al, what's going on? I told Gabby to go to the site and to be my eyes and ears."

"Ms. Phylis, I can't let anyone on da site widout proper construction boots."

Syliva –"Is this a law? Please cite the chapter, section and sub-section and referenced paragraph of the statute."

Al: "I doesn't know what yous talking about but I can tell yous that if an inspector comes by and sees your gal wid dem shoes, he's gonna have a problem which gonna be yuz."

Sylvia: "Well, you know more about this than I do; but please let Gabby use the ladies room."

She hangs up. Al gingerly escorts Gabby over wood planks to the temporary site toilets.

Gabby: "And what's this?"

Al: "Dez is da terlits wez got" as he opens the door to a vacant one. Gabby enters: "There's no mirror. No lighting. Do do I put my handbag? Oh my God; the smell! Yech, this is disgusting!"

Retching, Gabby exits. She's green and about to faint. Al grabs an unwrapped camphor disc and waves it under nose.

"Oy gevalt!" Gabby screams. "Get me the hell out of here!"

Then Hai Guy, owner of Sky Hai Cranes, drives on to the site. The front and back bumpers of his massive SUV spells out in large glowing letters: Visually Impaired Driver – Watch Out.

Al sees him: "Hi Hai – how's yis doin'?"

Hai uses a modified lift to lower himself from the cab.

"I gots duh talles sky crane in nort americas. Where's does yis want me to place it?"

Al: "Yis puts it over dare."

The construction site becomes very, very active, like what you see when you lift up a rock and see bugs running around underneath it. The project is running 24 hours a day in three eight hour shifts, sort of. Special piles are driven down towards the core of the earth. The drilling noise is deafening. Miles below the surface, hundreds of tons of concrete are poured and anchored to steel piles as Al's built a concrete mixing plant on site. Hai's tower cranes lift concrete transit mixing trucks to places that need concrete. Sylvia, through her connections, has had the Building Department, testing agencies and labs relocated and moved on to site as well. Inflated rats show up as a demonstration of the non-union construction and are being shot by Al's hired marksmen. The union reps are smart though; they have those 40 foot rats made out of Kevlar to deflect bullets.

But don't mess with Al. He has rocket propelled grenade launchers the marksmen use to blow the face off the multiplying rats as quickly as they're inflated. Al's set up a temporary construction trailer for meetings where there's always a pot of bitter thick coffee brewing. Taped to the wall is the construction schedule. Next to the schedule is a large calendar featuring 'The skimpily clad model' of the month. The calendar has been looked through many times and is already dog-eared. On the other side are large first aid kits and hard hats. In the middle of the trailer is a large card table surrounded by folding chairs. All sorts of permits and safety notices are taped to the wall. At one end of the trailer is a private office for Al who sits in a reclaimed, torn soft reclining chair. Al has pasted his favorite pictures of animals he's hunted next to nude centerfolds on his walls. Next to his desk is a 55 gallon drum of antacids.

Meetings are held weekly on the same day and start promptly at 7:00 a.m. Woody attends each meeting and takes the minutes. Al provides a large box of crème filled chocolate sprinkled doughnuts. The weather starts to become very cold as fall turns into winter. Gabby shows up from time to time wearing protective sheeting over her mink coat, new construction boots which her shoe maker dyed pink and added tiny heels and sequins to stay fashionable. She stays behind the scenes since has no idea of what's going on. The trailer's filled with contractors of different trades all having separate arguments about the past weekend's pro football game.

"He shulda trown da pass to Giantism, no ta Whaleovman.'

Big Tuna's describing the issues he had drilling through the earth's core. He's hard to understand since he's missing every other tooth and his tongue flaps around outside his mouth when he speaks:

"Al, iyes smitten a Change Oder fur da exra hard shafs I had ta buy. Just then the door to the trailer flys open. It's Les!!

"Well! Hello to all you strong men. I'm Les Ismore, the Starchitect and I just stopped by to make sure you realize who conceived of this baby! I did; this building has Les Ismore's signature on it!"

Woody looks over at Les, trying to hold back his thoughts. Then Les, looking at the group sitting around the table, says:

"Can I have a café latte with whip?"

The contractors have no idea what a café latte is.

Woody: "Les; why are you here?"

Les: "Voody; I want everyone to know this building was my idea! This was my idea! It was *my* idea, not yours. The Way I've been treated is intolerable and I'll make sure my publicist knows this."

Les starts sucking his thumb and takes part of his fur-lined cape, holds it next to his face and whimpers. Gabby is in awe.

"Mr. Ismore, I heard so much about you in my one day class at decorators school. Can I have your autograph? I saw the line of wire coat hangers you designed; WOW!"

Les: "SiSister, designing that line almost killed me. I fusssed and fussssed over the right shape sso it can ssslide along the rod just right. What's your name sweatheart?"

"Gabby Blabla" she responds.

Les: "Oh for heavens sssake, you did the Pinchers' apartment, didn't you?" Gabby nods yes.

Les: "Penny Pincher and I lunch each week at The Macadam (blacktop) Beach Club. Did you have the pleasure of working with her hedge fund husband, Doberman?"

Gabby nods yes. All of a sudden Al starts yelling:

"Take yis yakkin' outside; wez gay ah buildin' ta build."

The conversation around the table is somewhat disorganized as Woody reads the minutes taken from the previous meeting while Al tries to herd the 'cats.' Grunty

Fawcett, the plumbing contractor who wears his loose fitting pants that hang very low under his large stomach so when he bends over, you can see the crack in his ass, is huffing and puffing.

"I tried putting da sleeves in da pour forms and da fricken rebar . . ."

Al cuts him off: "Grunty, yuz looks flushed. Yyuz ah rite?"

Grunty: "I had da hot sausage an peppers hero. It boint goin' in and its gonna boint goin' out!!! Yuz got any antacids?"

Al: "Eis got dem in my erfice; hep yur sef."

Grunty: "An da fricken rebars too clos fur da sleeves."

Every day, contractors show up at the trailer with questions, complaints and clarifications about the scope, site access, coordination and a host of other issues as the building's flying up with a new floor being added daily as the window installation follows a few floors below. All of a sudden both Woody 's and Al's cell phones ring simultaneously. It's Sylvia.

"I'll calling to let you know I'll be at the project site tomorrow morning with my bankers and financiers. I expect everything to be in pristine condition. Thank you."

Woody looks at Al. You think this site is in pristine condition ? This is an active construction site. Al quickly leaves the trailer and gets to the middle of the site, takes out an air horn and a megaphone. He activates the air horn with multiple loud blasts then using the mega phone announces:

"Listen up! All of yuz! Tamarra, de owner's comin' hea wid ah buncha o'suits. Get yuz shits together!"

The next day, a black stretch limousine shows up. It's filled with men wearing dark stripped suits, white shirts and conservative ties. Sylvia, who had gone to the beauty parlor first thing that morning, had her hair and nails freshly done. She wears a multi-colored dress and super large hat. Al meets them.

In her loud voice, Sylvia says:

"Gentlemen; this is Al Dente. He's in charge of this project. Any questions, ask either him, or Woodward Kisser, who's the architect." She turns to Al.

"Okay, Al; it's your show; please proceed."

Just then, Les swoops in.

Les: "Welcome, welcome to my masterpiece. I'm Les Ismore, the starchitect who conceived of this building."

Sylvia frowns:

"Capeman, please, we don't have much ti . . ."

Les: "Have you boys seen the cover of 'Oooou," the mag of sheer style; I am the feature."

Sylvia: "Al, please take care of Capeman."

Al: "Hey twinkle toes; move ya ass aside" as the group moves towards the trailer. Once inside, Al says:

"Okay,yiz listen up. Yiz got ta change yiz fancy slippers fer deez boots, so select yis size. Den, yiz puts a hardhat on yis lid and den will take the hoist up ta da top."

The group gets into the temporary construction elevator which is on the outside of the building and starts its climb to the top of the floor that finished. A very strong wind is whistling through the hoistway cab as it rises, shaking, grinding and rattling. No banker has ever been in one of these before and they're frightened. One of the bankers asks the elevator operator:

"Is this safe?"

The operator responds: "Safe from what?"

At five hundred feet up, some in the group start to feel acrophobia and reach into their pockets for relaxants. The elevator operator announces:

"Folks; wez oly a sixteenth dah way ta deh top" and then the cab jerks to a stop. The operator says:

"Okay; bras, girdles and undies; all out," not realizing that Sylvia is in the group. Exiting the cab, the bankers stay clustered in a tight group, buffeted by the wind, holding hands and each other, as they walk around protruding rebar, core forms and workers. One banker says:

"Talk about being high; whew!"

The bankers gather for a group shot with Sylvia in the middle. Some are so nervous that you can hear their knees knocking. After the photograph, they all head quickly towards the elevator cab like elephants on parade. The ride down isn't quite as harrowing but the riders nonetheless are praying. Once back on terra firma, it's a different story.

"Aw! That was great; what views. Sylvia, this is fantastic!"

As they exit the trailer after changing back to their street shoes, Les comes prancing over:

"Isn't it absolutely magnificent? And wait till you see the crystal chandelier I selected for the lobby. The lighting does wonders for your skin tone. Here's a few of my business cards to give to your clients."

On the card is a large star with Les Ismore at its center. One of the bankers asks:

"Mr. Ismore; I didn't get the starchitect reference. What is that?"

Les: "Aren't you cute to ask? I only work on notable projects. I'm a conceptualist of aesthetic form, function and finishes; especially wallpaper. I have clients all over the worl . . ."

The banker interrupts.

"I've got to get to the car but you haven't answered my question. What is a starchitect?"

Les: "It's a . . . ah . . . ah . . ."

Sylvia: "Gentlemen; let's go. We have business to do."

During the ride back, the banker who asked Les the question he never got an answer to, queries Sylvia:

"Ms. Philis; can you explain what a starchitect is?"

Sylvia: "You all know my ex. He's always impressed by names, particularly the public when it comes to their homes. Me, well, I'm impressed by results; not names."

Turning to the cramped confines of the limousine, she asks the group:

"Did you ever hear of Les Ismore or even a starchitect? I certainly hadn't. So I did my due diligence. A starchitect is a term which has no legal basis and through my research, I've learned that the label developed in order to elevate some architects to a higher stature in the media, as if to say they design better residential buildings. I can't tell the difference, other than that the prices seem higher. I could call Joe Schmo a starchitect, you know? The term starchitect is used primarily for marketing and public relations purposes. I think of it as a miracle of marketing. Any other questions?"

One of the bankers then speaks.

"Ms. Phylis, prior to our meeting, I was doing some research myself. Are you familiar with the architect Deeh Itie? He was in the newspapers a few days ago and I looked him up online."

Sylvia pulls out her mobile phone and does a search on Deeh Itie. He's listed as 'The World's Greatest Starchitect' and she reads further. Those who live in Deeh Itie's building do not age, are always happy, etc., etc., etc. Sylvia is now very interested since she just had a face lift and other cosmetic procedures and would like to maintain her 'youthful appearance,' be happy and free of any medications she takes. She looks at a few of his buildings online and they are definitely different from what she's ever seen before. The most unusual use of forms, spaces, natural resources, colors, textures, collagen air induction systems, and technologies she's never heard of, all has her very intrigued. Sylvia's thinking: 'What a wonderful way to live. Deeh Itie's brought apartment living to a new standard.'

Sylvia sends an electronic message to Deeh Itie. "Please contact me; I want to talk to you ASAP. Sylvia Philis, Esq."

Woody gets Sylvia's message and many others. What does he do now? What would Sylvia think if he showed up as Deeh Itie? He decides to call God. God answers.

God: "Woody, I hear panic in your voice. What's going on?"

Woody: "You created this crazy website and now I'm being contacted."

God: "Isn't that what you wanted?"

Woody: "Yes …er… No… Yes …but – I don't know that I can deliver a building that has the systems and living conditions that you list on your website. And what do I do now that Sylvia Philis has contacted me?"

God: "Woody, it's your website that I created, not mine and I have two simple responses that I need you to absorb and think about. One: 'What the mind can conceive, man can achieve. Two: Become someone new; take on a new identity. You did ask me to make a big splash for you, didn't you?"

Woody: "I did, but I didn't think ahead of time about the challenge that confronts me now. And, take on a new identity? How am I supposed to do that?"

God: "Was air conditioning common in homes 150 years ago? What about light bulbs? Or even elevators or microwaves? C'mon Woody, step up to what you perceive as a challenge and embrace it. You'll have a wonderful, stimulating and provocative life experience. As for taking on a new identity, clean up your act, buy different clothes, grow a moustache or beard, dye your hair a different color and don glasses or something else. You figure it out."

Woody hangs up and researches make-up artists on line. There are many. Woody sees one – Pat's Body Shop - that has a most compelling website. He makes an appointment. They meet in Pat's overly cramped small office. The walls are plastered with photos of men and women. Many of the before photos are completely different from the after photos. Pat is a mildly attractive large woman who has had what appears as lots of cosmetic surgery. Pat also has a protruding Adam's apple. In her baritone voice, Pat asks:

"So Woody, why are you hear?"

Woody: "I need a new identity, whatever that is. Can you tell me a little about yourself?"

Pat: "I was formerly a plastic surgeon and …eh…I… eh… left the profession."

Woody: "You quit being a plastic surgeon - why?"

Pat isn't one to hide things: "I lost my license to practice when a lawyer came in for a nose job. I didn't like him so I replaced his nose with boar's snout. He also asked me to do hair transplant since he was balding so I took skin sections from his very hairy ass and graphed them to his head and then called him 'Shithead.' The only thing missing from the top of his head was remnants of toilet paper. Since he had connections and was very nasty, he had my license revoked so I turned to remaking myself which I did."

Woody: "Wow, what a story! Anything else?"

"Well, at one point in my life I was a male. But since my childhood, I always thought I was girl, I played with dolls, and even wore a brassiere under my clothes and carried sanitary napkins in my pocket, went through a sex change and, well . . . anyway, you only live once and I'm very happy now. I found this very unusual fellow who developed a website for me and helped me create 'Pat's Body Shop' and since then business has been booming. I still do facial changes and add fillers and 'body putty' where needed. I'm like an auto repair shop: they do frame alignment, I do nose alignment; they do dent and scratch repair; I fix cellulite and bad skin, et cetera. Now, how can I help you?"

Woody:" I have a dilemma. Can you help me become two people?"

Pat:" I don't understand. Please explain."

Woody: "Well for starters, I'm an architect and through my own insecurities, have pursued 'a below the horizons' profile and have become known as the architect of record for many developers. As a result, I end up making starchitects' concepts work. I now happen to be the architect of record on the largest residential condominium building ever constructed in the world. It's 8,000 feet tall and will include 600 hundred apartment units."

Pat: "Good grief, who would ever want to live in such a building."

Woody: "People with a lot of money who don't live there."

Pat: "What? That's crazy, but not your problem. Why the request for the two identities?"

Woody: "Have you ever heard of the term 'starchitect'?"

Pat: "No – what is that?"

Woody: "Well, it's a term developed by slick marketing gurus and real estate brokers to create the illusion that a starchitect's name creates better residential buildings. It's all hype. Most new residential buildings are all the same. Have you ever heard of the expression: '10 pounds of shit in a 5 pound bag'?"

Pat: "Of course . Why?"

Woody: "Think of a starchitect as one that puts the bow around the bag."

Pat: "Got it. A bow, probably pink, around a bag of shit. So what does that have to do with you?"

Woody: "I met this guy called God and he developed a website that turns me into a starchitect."

Pat: "So you want to be in that group that puts pink bows around bags of shit?"

Woody: "No! God has fabricated claims about residential buildings I have purportedly designed under the pseudonym Deeh Itie."

Pat: "Such as…?"

Woody:" Such as that residents live better, healthier lives; vitamins, collagen, testosterone and other life essentials come through the ventilation system and you liv…"

Pat interrupts: "Sounds fantastic; I'd go for that."

Woody: "Now I'm getting requests from people who know me and want to meet with me, but I'm still involved with the other building. I can't be the same person. Do you understand?"

Pat: "Sort of. What I'll do is create a mask and outrageous outfit you can wear to hide your natural appearance when you meet with anyone interested in Deeh Itie. You should consider getting a voice changing box, Okay?"

Woody: "Great!"

Just then Woody's mobile device vibrates. It's a contact from the world'sgreateststarchitect website, and it's from Rapid Pharma. Please call Dr. Derma Titus who's head of

Rapid's Research Department. Woody calls and hears in an Indian accent:

"Hellloo, Dis is Doctor Titus; with whom do I have the pleasure of speaking?"

Woody: "This is Woo...ah.. Deeh Itie. I received a message to contact you."

Dr. Titus: "Ah, yes Mr. Itie. Dr. Rippin Biter, the CEO and President of Rapid Pharmaceutical saw your website and wondered how you deliver collagen, testosterone and other pharmaceutical agents though your air delivery system. He has asked me to meet with you. Are you available to do so?"

Woody: " Ah....yes."

Dr. Titus: "Where's your office located? Can you give me three dates and times available?"

Woody: "Dr. Titus, I think it best I visit you. 'I'm working on confidential projects and our office is limited only to those whose projects we're working on." (Bullshit !!! – the only thing Woody has is a man cave.)

Dr.Titus: "Okay. We'll send one of our corporate jets to pick you up. Where are you located?"

Woody: "H*amada, hamada, hamada*...in the big city."

Dr. Titus: "Mr. Itie, wonderful. Please arrange to be at our corporate terminal at the airport at 6:00 am where we'll pick you up and fly you to our headquarters where you'll meet with Dr. Biter."

Woody dons his new identity which includes his mask, tattered robe with rope belt and sandals. Since he never paid attention to cutting or cleaning his overgrown, funky toenails or washing his feet, let alone his body, he fits the image Pat created. He boards the corporate jet as the only passenger. There's one flight attendant. The two pilots look back and wonder if they're transporting Osama bin Laden. He certainly smells like it. The flight attendant, wearing an oxygen mask and air fresheners as earrings, asks him if he'd like something to drink.

Deeh Ittie responds: "Natural tea made from vanishing glacial water steeped with conifer needles gathered above the tree line and served with a hint of goats sap."

'Deeh Ittie' is digging this new identity. The pilots are wondering if he ever changed his underwear or took a bath as they also put on oxygen masks as well. Once on the ground, Deeh Ittie's whisked by security to the conference room outside Dr. Biter's office. Deeh Ittie sits at a long inlaid veneer conference table with seats that can accommodate 30 with microphones. Large screen monitors with world clocks above surround the walls. It's a war room. Dr. Biter enters.

"Hello. I'm Dr. Rippin Bitter and I assume you are Deeh Ittie."

Deeh Itie fusses in his chair.

"Let me get straight to the point. I find the delivery of pharmaceuticals through your air system quite intriguing. Please answer the following: 1) How do you do it? 2) How do you control the amounts? and 3) How do you get access to the various pharmaceuticals delivered through your air system? I see this as a new distribution model for our drugs and Rapid shareholders will be frothing at the mouth to be in on the action."

Deeh Itie: "I cannot answer questions or divulge my sources."

Dr. Biter: "Mr. Deeh Itie, I assume you know who I am and the power I yield and please do not underestimate my extensive resources or people in high places that owe me favors."

Dr. Biter calls in Dr. Hal Atosis, Head of the Oral Care Division and Dr. Ben Diaz Epine, Anxious Mind Division in an effort to put more pressure on Deeh Ittie.

"Mr. Deeh Ittie! I will ask you my questions once again. 1) How do you do it? 2) How does your system control the amounts? and 3) Who supplies you with the various pharmaceuticals that get delivered through your air systems?

Deeh Ittie's cool and answers: "Drs. Biter, Atosis and Epine, Okay. I will answer your questions but the answers are quite abstract and you'll have to figure them out. He takes a marker and writes at the top of the white board:

Foxtrot, Uniform, Charlie, Kilo, Yankee, Oscar, Uniform.

"Now please return me to whence I came. Thank you."

Rapid security escorts Deeh Ittie back to the tarmac. The three doctors sit there very puzzled, scribbling away and somewhat happy to have the basis for the answers. Deeh Itie's on board the corporate jet. The flight attendant has an air sickness bag hanging around her neck. At Rapid, the three doctors continue to research various chemical formulas that that can be broken down into vapors while still retaining their potency. Biter calls in Indian code talkers, other scientists and a decipherer of smoke signals. The conference white board is covered in skeletal structural formulas, scribbles and diagrams. The mailroom messenger stops off to deliver important documents and sees the heading on the white board. ***Foxtrot,Uniform,Charlie,Kilo,Yankee,OscarUniform*** and blurts out.

"Wow! Uoah! I sees yoos einsteens tryin' to develop a pill to makes peoples say 'Fuck you!' Dat's COOL!"

Everyone in the room stops what they're doing and motionless, stares at the white board.

Dr. Biter: "Son, what did you say?"

Rasheed: "Son ? I isn't your son."

Dr. Biter: "I apologize. I couldn't read your name tag. I believe it's upside down. Will you accept my apology?"

Rasheed, under his breath says "Fuckin' honky' " I duz."

Dr. Biter: "What training did you have that gave you insight into what we thought was a compounded formula"?

Rasheed: " I was in da' amie, 68 tango."

Dr. Bitter: "And that would be?"

Rasheed: "Animal Care Specialist."

Dr. Biter: "What? How did you know that foxtrot, dingo, whatever, meant 'fuck you'?"

Rasheed: "Dat's da basic amie afabet, youz got ta know it ta pass da class. Udderwise day make youz runs around da track holden upa rifle ah da."

Dr. Biter's thinking 'We've been had.'

Deeh Ittie now goes back to being Woody who returns to his office. There's a pile of shop drawings stacked against his entrance door. He quickly goes through them, stamping them with a 'Received Dater.' He's got lots of messages asking him to call Sylvia, Al Dente, collection agencies, and many others. The most interesting one is from Moaner:

"Woody, I thought I'd let you know that I'm tired of just being considered a 'piece of meat,' some one's arm candy or the 'stunner in stilettos.' I've traded in my thongs for grannie panties; my mini-skirts for pants suits; tossed away my razor and no longer wear any make up. I've got a very capable brain and I'm going to use it. Everyone's getting into the development pool which is where I'm going to make a cannonball splash. I can yell, scream and pound my fist on the desk like the best of them and I can even not pay my bills. Look at Sylvia Philis. Now's she's developing the SaturnScraper and even changed its name to the Schnutzy after her pocket pooch. What's so difficult??? Why did my parents named me Moaner, I'll never know. What were they thinking? I've been made fun of all my life. 'Who's making ya moanin?' Do you believe that?I heard that so many times. It's so humiliating! Now that I'm in the real estate development business, I plan on succeeding, without the 'casting couch.' See my new website: www. buildit and she will come. com. Bye."

Woody thinks: 'Good for her. Just one more to add to the shark tank.' Woody then calls Sylvia and the conversation goes like this:

"Woodward, I want to meet with you and the Floral Capeman. I've researched this starchitect called Deeh Itie whose buildings seem very interesting. They're the current rage, in fact. They're designed to promote healthy living, yada, yada, yada, so come over here to my office right now!"

A few hours later, both Woody and Les show up at Sylvia's office and are escorted in the 'rococo gone mad' conference room. Sylvia says:

"I've tried to contact Deeh Itie but he hasn't responded. Are either of you familiar with his work?"

Woody remains motionless as Les pipes up:

"Sylvia – I think that flo . . ." Sylvia interrupts:

"Are we on a first name basis?"

"I'm sssory Ms. Philis, in any event, I think that Deeh Itie's projeccctss are hype and I sccertainly wouldn't beschmurch another professional but I know that my clients absssoluutely love my desssigns and my very fine touccchess - to say nothing about my guacamole and sunflower seed inssspired wallpap . . ."

Sylvia cuts him off: "I want to know what systems this guy Deeh Itie uses in his buildings that make them so popular. And I don't believe it's the guacamole and sunflower seed inspired wallpaper. Good day, gentlemen."

Woody and Les leave together. Les says to Woody:

"I can't believe this. Everyone loooves my buildings. Who else has edible wall paper in elevators? I'm just sooo creative and novel. If you get the munchies while you're in the elevator, you just tear off a piece and eat. What about my pre- stained carpet designs that hides 'the little furry one's 'got to go moment' or my multi-colored lipstick and eye shadow hallway appliqué with mirrors so you can do your makeup after you leave your apartment and while you wait for an elevator. What could possibly be better? How dare Deeh Itie think hees's so special ? I'll ssssea you later."

Les leaves to other destinations unknown. Meanwhile Woody gets another message forwarded from the 'theworldsgreatsstarchitect.com' website. It's from Sylvia.

"I want to talk to you. Please call me ASAP" and she leaves her contact number. Woody, feeling the pressure to talk to Sylvia in a tone she doesn't recognize, researches voice changing devices, purchases one and calls her.

"Helloo, I am calling for Sylvia Phylis, this is Deeh Itie."

Deeh Itie's voice is so low that the receptionist answering the call feels her ear drums' vibrate. She forwards the call to Sylvia.

"Ms. Philis, a Mr. Deity is on line 1, shall I transfer the call?

Sylvia: "Yes."

"Mr. Itie, I saw your website and am particularly interested in the claims that the residents in your buildings live happier, healthier and stress-free lives, among other things. I'd like to talk to you about a condo project I'm currently involved with."

Deeh Itie in a very deep toned voice says: " Ms. Philis, I have very sensitive hearing. I ask you, respectfully, can you please not yell when you speak?"

Sylvia is astonished. She thinks 'Who does he think he's talking to?' as she fiddles with the burdizzo in her free hand. But Sylvia's a smart woman and will play along so she tones down the volume and intensity.

"Mr. Itie, can we meet? I'd like to come to your office and see your projects; of course at your convenience."

Deeh Itie: "I think it best that I come to you."

Woody changes into his Deeh Itie outfit including his voice box and shows up at Sylvia's office where the receptionist is quite taken aback as she first sees him, saying: "Messengers are to use the delivery entrance and be checked in by security."

Deeh Itie plays along to keep the image effect and enters the secured area. One of the guards thinks to himself, as he wands Deeh Itie: "Whew, this guy got a dead animal in his pants." Once through, he's led back to the reception area where the receptionist is spraying the space with disinfectant and then escorts Deeh Itie into the 'rococo gone mad' conference room. The receptionist calls Sylvia:

"The 'second coming' is waiting in your conference room for you. Sylvia enters. She's taken aback as well but controls her reaction to Deeh Itite's appearance where she jokingly says:

"Where is the halo? So you're Deeh Itie. It's my pleasure to meet you. Can I offer you something?"

Deeh Itie answers in keeping within his character:

"Natural tea made from vanishing glacial water steeped with conifer needles gathered above the tree line and served with a hint of goats sap."

Sylvia's fast. She says: "I'm so sorry. We are currently out of that sap; it's extremely popular here. Would simple 'burled' tap water and lemon be of interest?"

Deeh Itie: "That'll be fine; thank you."

Sylvia: "I want to get down to business. Just to recap, I took over the development of the largest condominium residence that will ever have been constructed from my former husband Sy Philis. I don't know if you've ever heard of him. However that may be, he had a plan to build 10,000 units in a residential tower 8,000 feet tall. He hired a starchitect, Les Ismore who conceived of this crazy concept but knows nothing about construction or how things work or go together or anything else other than wearing ballet shoes. Ismore's more of what I would call 'Today's fashionable residential stylist' with his edible wall paper, imported fake flooring and mirrors that make fat people look skinny. Anyway, Sy also hired an architect of record to prepare the documents and to make things constructible. The two are ying and yang. His name is Woodward Kisser. The building's currently under construction; it's up to, I believe somewhere around 200 sores or 3,500 feet, and I'm already having agita with air traffic control. I have an on-site construction representative named Al Fresco, no, er, Al Risotto, or, uh, no his name is Al Fusilli . . oh, I'm having a senior moment . . . Al Dente – that's his name. He runs the job for me, but in any event, your buildings are so interesting and I've heard the residents living in them do not age, become medication-free and are always happy. How do you do it?"

Deeh Itie: "Ms. Philis, I do not give away my ideas. Clients hire me and I go forth and design."

Sylvia: "Well I want you to meet with Woodward Kisser and the so-called 'starchitect' Les Ismore and see if some of your ideas can be incorporated into my building."

Deeh Itie's now in a jam: "Ms. Philis, I cannot accommodate your request, I have . . ."

Sylvia interrupts: "Mr. Deeh Itie, no one says "No" to me. Here. I'm going to write you this check for one million dollars to be considered a retainer. I'll have my secretary arrange for a meeting between you, Kisser, Ismore and myself to discuss how we are to work together and make this building better. And now, I have another matter to attend to. Thank you." She eyeballs the burdizzo in her hand and then leaves.

As Deeh Itie is exiting, the receptionist, wearing rubber gloves and a hazmat suit asks for his business card so she can contact him later for the meeting.

Deeh Itie: "Please contact me through my website. I don't carry business cards. It's a waste of paper, paper which comes from trees. You should be concerned about saving the world."

The receptionist's thinking: 'This one should be on a late night reality show: "Weirdos You Never Knew Existed.'

Deeh Itie changes back to Woody who has to hurry up to the building site. There's lots of activity and Al Dente has lots of questions. The first meeting is with the elevator manufacturer along with a jet propulsion consultant, Schmitty, who speaks with a southern drawl and chews tobacca:

"Scheahms to me, we gotcha, what watcha call ah damn moon shot wid yur dee-signs. Us fellas at da lab" (Splat!) "liken what wesa see'in yur ideahs and mighty proud to be part of yur vision ." (Splat!) I spoke ta Schtumpy 'Fire in da Hole' Pyromania who'd be r techie on dis an he wants ta put some xtra hot sauce in the lift off ta make da travelin' experience sumptim special." (Splat!)

Woody: "What about the restraining devices?"

Schmitty: "Well, den we got thisa here a udder fella named Skinny who formerly worked in the contour panty hose business and he's knows lots about holden back expanding an' trusting forces. Schkinny's da man. Schkinny designed da frabric dat holds da jets landin on a flat top if da 'bolter'. He can make an elephant look like a geeraffe."

Just then Silvia shows up.

"Woodward, I want to speak with you. I met with Deeh Itie. He's very, very strange, quite odiferous, but I imagine very creative and I want you, Les and myself to meet with him and see what we can do to enhance this building's marketability. I don't think the edible elevator wallpaper has much of a shelf life. Please keep your schedule flexible, as my secretary will be in touch with you. And Al, be sure to update me."

Woody leaves. He gets a prompt on his mobile device from the worldsgreateststararchitect.com website. It's from Sylvia's secretary requesting his presence at a meeting in her office next Tuesday at 1:00 pm. Moments later he gets an email from Sylvia's secretary requesting his attendance at the same meeting. Woody's now got a significant problem.

The following Tuesday, at 1:00 pm, Woody and Les Show up at Sylvia's office and are led into the now all too familiar conference room. Sylvia walks in:

"Where's Deeh Itie? We can't start the meeting without him."

1:15 is followed by 1:30, 2 p.m. and 2:30. Finally, Sylvia belts out to her secretary:

"Dottie Whitehead, did you make contact with Deeh Itie?"

Dottie: "All he gave me was his website to contact him on."

Sylvia: "What? You have no phone number of e-mail address for him?"

Dottie starts to shake knowing Sylvia proclivity to use her burdizzo when pissed off even though it might not directly apply to her.

Dottie: "Ms. Phylis, I will make every attempt to contact him again."

Sylvia turns to Woody and Les:

"Thank you both for showing up. We'll reschedule."

She walks out.

Les says to Woody: "Oi figured as sssooo. I knew he wasn't going to ssshow up. He's afraid of me."

Woody thinks: 'I wonder what drugs Les takes?'

Woody then goes back to his home office, his man cave. On the way back he purchases the cheapest cell phone he can buy and he now has an established number which he can use under the pseudonym of Deeh Itie.

Once in his office, he establishes a simple email for Deeh Itie; ditie@deehItie.com while his other mobile device has been pulsing after receiving numerous requests from developers all over the place who have seen his worldsgreateststararchitect.com website. He also gets another message from Dottie Whitehead requesting his email address and phone number, which he responds to now that he has both.

Dottie promptly responds back requesting his attendance for a new meeting date, next Tuesday at 1:00 pm. Deeh Itie confirms. Dottie then sends out the same request to Woody and Les. It takes a while but both confirm as well. Sylvia checks in with Dottie.

"Dottie; are we all set for next week?"

Dottie affirms.

Meanwhile, Woody's got to keep up with and try to get ahead of the onslaught of shop drawings and requests and clarifications of information (RFI's) from the building contractors as the tower construction races skywards. The paint and wallcoverings submittals still get sent to Les.

Tuesday rolls around and at 1:00 pm, Deeh Itie shows up and is directed to the conference room. In preparation for this meeting, Les has stopped off at his favorite coiffure, had a touch up and arrives a few minutes late. He enters the conference room where he is completely startled by Deeh Itie's appearance and odor. Les reaches into his pocket and pulls out a little plastic box of small breath mints, many of which he stuffs into his nostrils. He then walks out and asks Dottie if she has surgical gloves;

she now happens to have a box of them. Les dons a pair and sashays back in, trying not to retch.

"Whew! Well, if the floor waz water, I'd ask you to walk on it!"

Just then Sylvia walks in scanning the room: "I guess we're now waiting for Woodard. 1:15, 1:30, 2:00 and they all sit there playing with their mobile devices, answering and sending emails, while every once in a while, Les makes a snide comment under his breath:

"Can you turn water into wine, Chumpsky?"

Sylvia's getting impatient.

"Dottie Whitehead; please get Woodward on the phone, right now."

Dottie: Ms. Phylis, I just received an email from Mr. Kisser that his car got caught in a sand storm and cannot make it."

Sylvia: "What the hell is going on? A sandstorm? Where is he, in the desert?"

Les, with arched eyebrows, steps in to gain traction and credibility with Sylvia:

"Mr. Itie, eyemah not at all familiar with your work. What do you think you can contribute to moy creashion?"

Deeh Itie: "I take a very different approach than I gather you do."

Sylvia's ears are perked as Les' nostrils are flared in contempt.

"I focus less, and I mean no direct insult to your name, on the type of kitchen counter tops, fancy ranges and imported fake veneer flooring, etc. and more on creating healthy habitation. The systems and environments I've designed understand the DNA of each resident; a simple example of this is my Itie Environaire system which captures all of the pollutants creating a dust free home while also keeping a balanced, even air flow system that eliminates drafts and keeps the volume of the living space, floor to ceiling, of the apartment at the same temperature; a more sophisticated system is the Itie Cankles Reduction Complex, Itie Resolution of E.D. Complex or the Itie Body Sculpting System or the Anxiety & Procedural Calming System ."

Sylvia's fascinated, Les is anguished. In a sweet, soft tone Sylvia says:

"Tell me more! Do the systems you've designed reduce crankles, eliminate turkey neck or deal with my five o'clock shadow?"

"They do. As you might know, my buildings also come with specially designed furnishings. Take bedding as an example. I've designed the pillow cases that have specifically infused collagen fibers which promote healthier skin and a breathing device that improves blood flow through inspiration and exhalation. Within the mattress there is the Itie leg compression device that keeps blood circulation at a constant rate and . . ."

All of a sudden, the batteries in his voice changing box starts to lose power and his diction changes, noticeably. He adjusts the scarf around his neck; it hides the voice box device.

"I don't feel that well and must leave right now."

Dieh Itie bolts.

Sylvia and Les are startled.

Sylvia: "Well, that was unfortunate. It must be something he ate. He certainly has different and creative ideas."

Les, trying not to lose his spot in the starchitect limelight, says:

"*Mon dieux*! I ssstill feel the clear plastic inflated toilet seets I designed, embedded with gold coins creating a toilet seet the 'throne of king and queens' makes everyone feel better when doing their 'business,' certainly has a lot going for it as well as *my* special 'Look How Good I Look' in my rose-tinted concave mirrors which can easi . . ."

Sylvia cuts him off: "Les, zip it! I want the residents of my building to be happy and have a life-enhancing experience. Dottie Whitehead, what's the latest with Woodward?"

Dottie: "I'll try him again."

She gets Woody: "Please hold for Ms. Phylis."

Sylvia: "Woodward; where are you that you're stuck in a sandstorm. I've never heard of anything like that?"

Woody: "I was driving behind one of those large transit mixers that used to deliver concrete, but it was loaded with sand and the back opened up and dumped its whole load on my car."

Sylvia: "Oh my God. Were you hurt?"

"No,not at all. I was on . . ."

Sylvia cuts him off: "Good. Woodward, I've got to get you, Deeh Itie, Ismore and myself together for a meeting right away. Itie's got some interesting ideas I'd like incorporated into my building. Make time for me."

Woody's in a terrific bind. He's between the rock and hard place. He's getting requests for meetings from many other developers who have seen his website and want their buildings to be uniquely special. The word is getting around. Deeh Itie has now become the world's greatest starchitect. The disguise Pat made for him is now becoming cumbersome. Woody's not comfortable with the character changing and the duplicity of being Deeh Itie and himself so he reaches out to God for advice but he gets no response.

Woody's becoming very worried, uncomfortable and very frustrated so he calls Dr. Thalamus who had originally diagnosed his brain tumor for an appointment to get a status update although he hasn't had any headaches. He finds out that the doctor retired. Woody has no one to turn to. He ponders his destiny. He wonders why he chose being stuck in a sandstorm as his lie to Dottie. Was that a metaphor for his life? And about what Dr. Thalamus said: '…think of each grain of sand as an aspect of time and fate'. What does he want in his life? Does he have what it takes to be recognized as a starchitect or more importantly, considered as one of worthy note, no longer the guy to go to that makes sure everything works but gets little credit? As Woody paces around, he's starting to create a circular wear pattern in the floor. What does he have to lose by exposing Deeh Itie's true identity?

Nothing!

Bravely, he calls Sylvia's office; Dottie answers.

"Dottie, this is Woody Kisser. I've got to speak to Ms. Phylis right away.

Dottie: "She's with a new client and has her burdizzo sharpener waiting."

Woody hears Sylvia yelling and screaming in the background.

"Dottie, you tell her that I've got Deeh Itie with me and this can't wait."

Sylvia gets on the phone.

"Woodward, what's up? I'm very busy?"

"Ms. Philis, I must see you right now."

"This better be damn important. Get to my office by 3:50 and not a minute later. I have only five minutes I can spend with you before my next appointment.

Woody shows up and is escorted you know where. Sylvia walks in, hands on her hips.

"What's so important that you need to see me on such short notice?"

Woody takes a deep breath and pauses.

"Ms. Phylis. I am Deeh Itie."

"*What* did you say?"

"I am Deeh Itie, really."

Sylvia's eyes widen, her mouth opens, she's stunned as she tries to maintain her composure while taking a seat on one of the Louis XIV chairs

"What? What are you talking about? What, what, what?"

She pulls out her burdizzo. Woody, sees it, grabs a chair and places it between himself and Sylvia.

"Ms. Phylis, your former husband hired me to be the architect of record for his building after he hired Les Ismore . As you probably are aware, Sy wanted a 'starchitect' to be associated with his project to further enhance the marketability since Les doesn't do anything other than concept design."

"I know he's really a cosmetician. Where did Deeh Itie come from?"

"Please don't hear this as if I'm casting aspersions on Les. For a building project to be successful, it has to go through a series of steps including the interface of the other consultants necessary to make the building work."

Sylvia's tapping in her foot in impatience.

"Woodward, I know, I know. Get to the Deeh Itie part, the costume, the voice, the smell!" She's fiddling with the burdizzo.

"Here's the thing. Being in this role of the architect of record has long frustrated me, so I met with God and he developed . . ."

"What? You met with God? Woodward, don't be silly with me. I'm an educated woman. I don't have time for this. Spare me, please!"

"Ms. Phylis, I didn't meet with the "God" you know. I met with this guy who calls himself God. He's just a website designer and he uses the name God since no one else uses it. He's unique and created a completely new branding image for me to elevate me to starchitect status. The response from his website design has been incred…"

"Are you telling me those buildings on the website with all those features are God's damn imagination and fictitious?"

Woody bows his head in contrition: "Yes."

"Oh my God. Not your God! So the part about residents in your buildings living healthier lives . . . is all of that possible, or is it B.S.?"

"I believe it's all possible."

Sylvia's mood is changing, slightly.

"Woodward, I had originally thought some of Dee Itie's ideas were quite novel. Now I understand they are just ideas. Can any of those features be added to my building? I'd like to have a building that enables residents to live happier, healthier, less stressful lives. Can you do it?"

Woody: "I certainly can. There are features that would make your building better. Some can be implemented immediately, others will need research."

"Woodward, I'm certainly not one to be duped. And you *do* know that expression "Don't learn to shave on my face,' don't you?"

She whips out her dulled-down burdizzo.

"Okay, listen Woodward. Give me two lists, features that can implemented now and those that need research. By the way, I'm somewhat curious to know about your opinion of this building, particularly the height. Personally, I think Sy wanted to build such a ridiculously tall building to compensate for his physical inadequacy."

"Ms. Phylis, I really can't comment on that. I think it best to get moving on making this building better."

"O.K., O.K., O.K. I can't be late for my next appointment. Let's get to work. I'll call Ismore and update him."

As Sylvia is leaving, she turns, waggling the burdizzo.

"Woodward, I always wondered about you. Oh well."

Later that day, Les calls Woody.

"Woody, this is Les. Are you trying to make a fool out of me? I knew all along that this Deeh Itie thing was a scam. Even my hair dresser told me as ssuch."

"Les, we have two ways to proceed with this project: **1.**We can be adversarial in the building progresses or **2.** We can be complimentary. You decide."

Les calms down: "As long as I get top billing, I won't be grandstanding."

Woody says: "Okay, but the credit for my ideas belongs to me and only me."

"Alright, as long as you don't use my signature poopoo platter designs."

Woody goes back to working on Sylvia's project. He starts researching all the luxurious features represented on the worldsgreateststararchitect.com website and what he can immediately issue as bulletins so they become part of the project. Of course, Sylvia *and* Les are copied as well.

Woody remembers his former college roommate Adam Baum who was a chemistry major. Quite innovative, almost genius level as Woody recalls while trying to locate him. Using different internet resources, he finds Adam. The two connect. Through emails, the communications go as follows.

"Adam; I hope you are well. I have fond memories of our college days. One memory was your ability to synthesize pot and LSD to making it odorless and have it distributed through the air ducts. Remember in the Art History class, the pretty girl who got so high, she took off all of her clothes and claimed she'd model for anyone, even if they couldn't draw or didn't have a pencil and paper or a camera. Crazy days. It's certainly been a long time. Too long. How are you?"

Adam responded: "Woody, you old pecker, good to hear from you. I recently got out of the slammer for blowing up the processing plant where they were reconfiguring waste products into baby food. As you might remember, I was a member of Students Unaware of Corporate Killings, Manufacturing Environmental Offensives Forgeries and Fraud. Now, I'm consulting to a start-up group that has a concept using toe cheese that become transformed into a new health juice. It's a far out concept but I think I can make it work. Are you still practicing in the 'Gentleman's Profession?' What prompted the email?"

Woody: "Yeah, I'm still at it. Adam, I was wondering if it's at all possible to convert conventional drugs or applications that are taken orally or applied topically to become delivered through an air system."

Adam: "Piece of cake."

Woody: "Do you have time to make a trip into the city? Or could I come to you? Whichever is easier."

Adam: "Let me check with my parole officer. I'm still wearing an ankle monitoring device, but I'll get back to you."

With that, Woody's confident that he can incorporate some of the website ideas into the building's systems. He goes back to the construction site. Al's got a new set of teeth that don't fit well in his mouth. They're too big, and when he talks, his choppers keep shifting, affecting his speech.

"Wooiudy, I gots a call froM Mrs. PhyLIS . ShE told MEs dar mIGht bEEs sum chnagEs comIN' down da ROad. Duz Ya know 'Bout dis?"

Woody: "I told Ms. Phylis that I was Deeh Itie and she'd like to incorporate some of his new and unconventional ideas into her building."

Al: "Who da' FuCK ah DeiTY?"

"Al, it's a long story, but I can tell you that there *will* be changes."

"WeLl dar 'stallin da windis aw'ready."

"Al. I'm working on that, as well as keeping up with torrent of shop drawings, bulletins and RFI's. Anything you want me to look at?"

"Na, yuz Drawins' is pretty daMn good. Let Me Ax ya, whad's wid dis stark architect bullshit I'm hearin'?"

"Al, you've been around the construction business for a long. long time and I believe you've had your moments of doubts and pains. Am I right?"

"Yeh."

"What might be confusing to you is the nature of the game."

"WhAt gaME? I'm bulLDin' a fuckin tall bulLDin' -- you tinK DIS is a gaME?"

"Not what you're doing, Al. It's the marketing of a building that's a game.

"HUH – wadDa talKIN?"

Woody: "Al, during your career, you've managed the construction of many high rise residential buildings both condos and rentals. Would you say that almost all residential buildings are the same, except for the finishes and furnishings?

"Yeh, bEEn dar, duN It."

When you worked for Sy Philis and he wanted to build this enormous tower with 10,000 apartments, he needed everything going for him, correct?"

"Wadda mean?"

"Other than it being a very tall tower, what do you think would make this building attractive to buyers?"

"I dunno kNow. My oLd LadY wouLDn't wANt ta live here. ShE's feeRed of heiGHTs and coULDn't give twO Shits 'boUT Seeing intA da CapitAl of RuskieLand."

"Well your wife might not be the targeted buyer, however most developers need something that makes their building's special and attractive, in addition to the location and the more of those 'somethings' include promoting that it's been designed by someone 'special.' That's the genesis of the term 'starchitect'."

"GeeZEE. Da wIfE wAs reAdin' da bIBle anD sHe wAS Tellin' 'bOut dA chapter on Genesis . . ."

Woody interrupts: "Al, let's move on already."

Just then he gets a call from Adam.

"Hey Wood, I've been experimenting with the idea of converting conventional drugs into a vaporized air delivery system and it fricken works."

"Holy shit, I thought it was just a crazy idea. Did you speak with your parole office about coming to the big city?"

"I did and as long as I call him every 90 minutes to tell him where I am, he'll be fine, although I still have to wear the ankle tracking device. Hey, I had another idea. Got a minute?"

"I'm all ears. Whatta' got?"

"How about a device you wear as a hat that receives signals from different areas of your brain and analyzes your state of being and makes mood adjustments accordingly?"

"I like that and believe many are working on a concept like that currently, but I've got to implement systems now."

"Okay. I'll get going on the various delivery systems."

Meanwhile, Woody's getting inundated with requests for meetings from developers around the world who have seen the website God created. His head is spinning. Where best should he best spend his efforts? The Schuntzy is now topped off at 8,000 feet and casts such a large shadow on South America that the coffee and cocoa plantations have no sunlight. Cocaine might end up being in short supply. The tuned mass dampener is installed to cut down on sway. The building sways only 12 feet in one direction. The rocket propelled elevators cause so much stack effect, female brokers cannot wear skirts or dresses since their panties come flying off due to the extreme negative pressure as the elevators rapidly ascend.

There's a sign in the elevator cabs:

> '***NOTE TO OCCUPANTS:*** *Plastic surgery fillers may temporarily deform due to acceleration. Use putty knives for adjustment. In the case of breast implants, please check your underwear.*'

Sylvia calls Woody.

"Woodard, how are you doing with those Deeh Itie "Better living" ideas? By the way, Dottie Whitehead just returned from the building. She said she as completely taken aback at its scale. She took one of the rocket-thrusting elevators to the penthouse floor. During the ride up, she had a deep pore facial cleaning. She no longer wants to be known as Dottie Whitehead."

"I'm glad she liked it. The life rejuvenation and ED accelerometer systems will be installed soon, along with some of the special furnishings that include collagen infused fibers, and so on."

Sylvia says: "I just hired the marketing firm Reamin & Skemin at Les's suggestion. He said Auger Reamin was one of the best, especially when he gets lubed up. I thought about using Jacques Strapp's firm, but he said his cup was overloaded and that he had too many balls in the air."

Meanwhile, Les has jumped the gun and has a story featured in a glossy fashion magazine. The cover story is titled 'Bathe With The Stars' and there's a slick picture of Les, lying prone in a chaise lounge, being sprinkled with star dust and glitter. In the article, Les takes all the credit for the building and makes no mention of the history of the project or project team. Les has even renamed The Schuntzy to The Starscraper.

Sylvia sees a copy at the newsstand, buys it and is completely stunned by the article. The next day as she's dressing, watching one of the morning news programs where they feature topical stories, she sees Les being interview by a television reporter. He sits in a chair with his cape and suave shades acting like his shit doesn't stink.

Sylvia blows a major gasket. She calls Les.

"Ismore, you certainly have a God-damn pair of balls! Did you get my permission to say anything to the press or media about *my* project? Who the hell do you think you're working for? And what's with changing the name of *my* building to The Starscraper? I'm thoroughly pissed off! Remember! I carry a special device in my purse that'll raise your voice 20 octaves higher."

Les in a very low, teary and yielding voice, holding his blanky says:

"Ms. Phyllis, I'm ssssooo sooorrry. I ssssertainly meant no disssrecpect. My good friend works at 'In Vain' mag and asssked me if I had anything newsworthy sssoo I said yesss."

Sylvia slams the phone down and is fuming. She calls Woody:

"Woodward, that fricken Capeman went ahead, without my permission, and had *our* project publicized. He even had the chutzpah to go on television and take all the credit."

"Ms. Phyllis, please calm down. It can't be all that bad. Look on the bright side. What he did will generate lots of attention for your building."

Sylvia is thinking, and thinking, before saying:

"Yeah, you're probably right. Woodward, you always maintain an even keel. I like you. Hmmm. Please call me "Sil" from now on. Mrs. Philis is just too formal. Can I entice you into coming over to my apartment tonight? I just ordered a case of rare vintage 1939 champagne and I hate to drink alone."

"Hama, Hama, Hama, I, er, I ah, er… ah… I have to get my knob polished, er . . . I mean I have to ah . . . to get special door knob polish."

Sylvia now speaks in a softer, more seductive tone:

"*Wood*ward, my cleaning lady and butler are away on vacation. I have cupboards full of many different types of polishes, ointments and jellies for all types of uses. Why don't you come over and look through my selection? You might be pleasantly surprised. Rrrrrrr . .. ."

Woody's imagining the skin folds of a pachyderm's butt and starts to stutter:

"Ah, er, Ms. Phylis, tttank you for your kkkkk-kind offer bbbbut I have to r-r-r-r-read the bbbb-building code t-t-t-tonight as well."

"Woody, c'mon now, the building code can wait and will still be there tomorrow. Come to Mommy."

Woody's getting an in-rection (a reverse erection).

"Ms. Phylis, please, we must keep our relationship strictly and only professional."

"Well okay, but you have *no* idea what you are missing."

Woody's thinking to himself: 'What I'm missing ? I certainly know what I'm missing. Good Grief! I just avoided an all out disaster. Woody remembers an awful, not-to-be-repeated-again college experience where he and a sorority fem, stoned and drunk, were going at it on a water bed, and got seasick, necessitating three days in recovery. Woody maintains his 'even keel' and gently disperses Sylvia's desire.

"I'll take you up on your invitation at another time but thanks for thinking of me"

Meanwhile the requests for meetings are still flooding in from developers from all over the world. The website God created is phenomenal. Woody decides to rid himself of his dowdy appearance and to remake himself in the image of a true starchitect.

He visits Pat, who helps to create the sartorial attitude for him. Woody heads to a clothing store frequented by high society people. He dons a black on black scheme without socks. It suits his new arrogant attitude perfectly.

Reamin & Skemin, meanwhile, are having a ball marketing The Schuntzy. Working with real estate brokers, there are daily trips by potential buyers to the building site where Al holds court. Next to the site is a prefabricated building within which is a mock-up of a model apartment. Woody has incorporated some of the life rejuvenating features in the model room. The interested parties leaving the mocked-up apartment feel suddenly different and quite sexually stimulated. One elderly couple who haven't had sex in years are overheard speaking to each other.

"Honey, you're looking at me in a way you haven't looked at me in years. There's desire in your eyes. You're holding my hand. What's going on?"

"Oh sweetheart, let's just go home right now before we lose the urge and get distracted by a reality TV show or that gallon of vanilla ice cream in the freezer."

The news media has picked up the story about the now transformed starchitect Woodard Kisser. Almost overnight, he's gone from being relatively unknown to celebrity status. He hadn't previously noticed that God had added highlights to the website claiming the world's greatest starchitect had won awards.

Woody receives an invitation from a nationally syndicated morning show for an interview, which and accepts. But he's scared shitless. He receives a supportive call from Sylvia who had heard that the world's greatest starchitect will be a guest on the morning show.

"Look, Woodward. Be known as Woodward, not Woody anymore. Woody is too casual a name for someone having elite starchitecture status. Be above it all.

By the way, I've decided to change the name of the building again to The Saturnscraper. The Schuntzy is too cute a name for a building."

Woody has never been in the public limelight before, let alone on television. He shows up at the station, nervous as hell, goes through the make-up procedure and sits across the self-assured and cosmopolitan reporter who welcomes him. Woodard is dressed the part of a starchitect. Black on black with black shades. The interview goes like this:

Reporter: "Mr. Kisser! Thank you for joining us this morning. I imagine you must have a very busy schedule with all the projects you have going on."

Woody, thinking the only project he has going on is The Schnutzy, now The Saturnscraper suddenly has an immobilizing brain freeze and answers: "Yes," as he clenches his fists and perspiration shows through the powdery face make-up. The reporter was looking for a longer answer and aware of the time limits of the interview, quickly interjects:

"I notice one of the claims on your website is that people living in the buildings you've designed are happier, become younger and live longer. The rush to live in your building must be enormous. What do you incorporate in the design of your buildings to create those wonderful conditions?"

"I can't divulge my secrets because they'll be copied by others wanting to make similar claims to the health and longevity of the residents."

Interviewer: "I understand and appreciate your pride of ownership. I have another question: your website notes that you're an award-winning architect. What awards have you won?"

Woodard's now so damn nervous, his thinking is 'upside down' but he's got to act cool in his new role of Starchitect." With all the pressure, though, he's creating an impression that he's on drugs.

"Oh, gosh, I'll mention a few: I received Le Casa de Mierda award; the Frutti di Mare award; the prestigious French award Tour Attrape Couillon; award for the speed of pitching a tent in the woods; I, ah, won an archery award in camp; another award I won . . ."

The interviewer tries to speak over the howling laughter of the camera crew behind the scenes but he's unsuccessful and so goes to commercial break. The interviewer gets up from his chair, shaking his head in disbelief as Woodard bolts out of the studio.

Back on the street, Woodard reverts back to his old mindset as he passes by a newsstand where he sees a tabloid in bold headlines:

SALES OFF THE CHARTS AT THE SATURNSCRAPER.

Woody's phone rings. It's Les.

"Voodward – are trying to sssuplant me ahss the starchitect on The Starscraper. I sshaw you on television. Nice outfit. Black on black is in until oi decccide differently."

"Les, the interview wasn't about The Starscraper, it was about . . ."

"Voodard, did you noticcce that Sylvia changed the name of my building to The Starscarper, the name *I* came up with?"

"Yeh, good 'bouy' for you. Look, I've got to get going so see you next time."

Les: "Just you wait one minute 'mmmiiisssssster'. I'm Les Ismore – Starchitect – I have the secret sauce and don't you forget it! And another th . . ."

Woody hangs up. Les immediately calls back.

"Another thing 'mmmiiisssssster', I saw you on television. I've won awards too. Did you know I received the prestigious 'Placard d'Elegance' for the wire coat hanger I designed? And the acclaimed **Adjudicacion Del Diseño Tonto** for my edible wall paper?"

Woody hangs up again.

The apartments at The Saturnscraper are selling like hot cakes and Sylvia couldn't be more pleased. The bankers are equally impressed. Seems like everyone who invested in the project is making money and Woody gets a nice check in the mail for his efforts.

The penthouse is sold for millions of dollars to a couple with acrophobia; a young woman with anuptaphobia, arrhenophobia and heterophobia buys an apartmen . Two guys buy an apartment; one has bogyphobia, the other has medomalacuphobia. Many other buyers have all sorts of unusual phobias and manias as well but their conditions and disorders will all be gone soon enough after living in The Saturnscraper, The news about all of benefits of living in The Saturnscraper go viral. Sylvia moves in and her cankles start to disappear.

An architecture critic writes, in part:

***

> "STOP THE PRESSES!!! The harmonic symphony of concrete, steel and glass boldly ignoring typology and the conventions of entablature or even applications of a single squinch have been artfully blended together in an ultra-magnificent composition of urbanity birthed in a spectacular and completely unheralded cosmopolitan edifice called The Saturnscraper. Without hyperbole I tell you that this building is, at present, insuperable. Where else on God's green earth is there a building that makes one's entire existence better simply by living in it? The complexity of the fenestration is

elaborate and uncompromising as it bows to no one. The finely aggregated architectural concrete pays respect to the virginity of its origin and the glass – oh my - as if it's non-existent. With raging hormones, The Saturnscraper stands alone without peers as witness to the combustion chambers propelling residents in rocket canisters to their destination elevating skyward towards the constellation Scorpius. Beckon oh Lord as I genuflect to its presence. As if transported to time unchartered, The Saturnscraper is everything past imagination. One is at a loss for the expected breathtaking views, but the unexpected amenities, suffice to say, are in another realm. Health and wellbeing, life extension, happiness, cures . . . you name it, are all masterfully realized in The Saturnscraper completely supported by the musculature of the building's viscera which by extension stakes claim to the manifesto, et cetera, et cetera.

***

And Woodward's on the road to presumed fame and fortune while Les' writes to the Editor-in-Chief complaining that his name's never mentioned in the article.

"Dear Ssthir: I read your extraordinary pieccce about The Saturnscraper in the very popular magazine for those with an IQ over 130 and I must say I was disappointed that my name was omitted. Just so you know – sstrhir – I am the starchitect who conceived of this building and think it's appropriate to give credit when credit is due. Thank you."

The critic writes back, faintly apologizing for his oversight and asks for more information about the building systems that deliver life-prolonging benefits. Les knows nothing about them or how they work.

"My Dear Starchitect Ismore: Please accept my sincerest apologies for the omission of your name to my erudition of your brilliant creation. The Saturnscraper is surely something to behold. As a follow-up, I'd like to write a piece on the wonderful life betterment systems you've incorporated in the building. Please elucidate further."

Kindest regards, Arbiter.

Les is at a total loss and can't respond. He had nothing to do with anything. other than developing a sketchy idea of the façade and rough interior layouts that didn't work. Woody did everything along with incorporating the genius of Adam Baum's medicinal delivery systems. It's as if Woody's created the fountain of youth. And this is making big news all over. Everyone wants 'in' on The Saturnscraper. Developers are rushing in to see this new miracle of a building. Sylvia, after living in The Staturnscraper, now has the same trim body she had when she was twenty. She discards her pantsuits, old lady shoes and pantaloons. Even her grey roots are gone. She's thrilled. In her newfound youthful excitement, she's about to join an on-line dating site but realizes she doesn't have to since there are many available prospects living in her complex. She has access to them via the building's own companion website www.starsinmyeyes.com. She does, however, still keep her burdizzo, as a memento.

The Saturnscraper is now completely sold out and occupied. Wow! Les enters The Saturnscraper in architectural competitions, without even a mention of Woody, and he's winning award after award. Woody sees the cover of one architecture magazine featuring the story of The Saturnscraper. It's also the cover story of numerous weekly news media publications.

***

> *'Starchitect, Les Ismore has created an alliance with the cosmos in the newest, most unusual residential condominium ever constructed. It's called The Saturnscraper. Ismore, known to many earthly stars, has created an 'out of this world' experience in the tallest, most compelling building that has ever shaped the planet's skyline.*

***

Woody's dismayed. Les is taking all the credit for The Saturnscraper, even though he, Woody, put his heart and soul into the project. But he's now inundated with requests from prospective developers who have seen 'theworldsgreatsstarchitect.com' website and are aware of The Saturnscraper. Woody has scheduled meetings for new projects and knows Les doesn't have a clue about the way a building really needs to work and function. With the money Sylvia paid him, he fixes up his office so it's more presentable. Woody's stride is different. He walks erect, head up and confident as he muses over the experiences he had pulling the project together and thinks about the various characters he has had to deal with along the way.

He's walking around and enjoying the nice weather when he suddenly and unexpectedly passes by the old dusty shop where he purchased the sphinctometer and other non-essential gadgets. He notices in the store front window a beautiful old hour glass on display. It has sand only in the top bulb and no sand in the bottom. Woody stands there and ponders it. He wonders if it works. The hour glass represents time standing still with only the future remaining and no past. Woody thinks back to the doctor he saw when he had his headaches which now occasionally return. The doctor used the hour glass with sand passing through the constriction point as a metaphor for the presence of life with each grain of sand having some meaning. At that time, as a result of the doctor's diagnosis, Woody decided to live his life to the fullest because the concept of mortality wasn't previously present in his daily thinking. But now with his new found fame, Woody's being recognized as the world's greatest starchitect and developers are requesting his services for projects.

Les calls him and asks if he would like to collaborate on some other projects; Woody says no.

"But Voody, we get along sthooo well and The Saturnscraper isths a sthmashing sucksuccess."

Woody: "I'm too busy with my own projects. Furthermore, I saw that you took all the credit and awards without even a mention of me and I'm the architect of record."

Les: "Oh Voody – my publicisthst made that mistake. I would *never*..."

Woody hangs up.

Soon, Woody's traveling around the country designing new, interesting and challenging projects, all the while bringing along the hour glass as a reminder of the future. Unfortunately, his headaches are increasing.

At each city where he has a new project, he stays in a five-star hotel. He's always certain to place the hourglass on a credenza in his room, always wondering why, exactly, all of its sand remains in the upper bulb. One night, though, after a very satisfying culinary experience with a client, he returns to his room, there seeing that all of the sand in the hourglass has fallen into the bottom bulb.

****

Edwards Brothers Malloy
Thorofare, NJ USA
February 4, 2016